THE TALONS OF A LYON

The Lyon's Den Connected World

Jude Knight

Dragonblade Publishing, Inc. is an imprint of Kathryn Le Veque Novels, Inc.

P.O. Box 23

Moreno Valley, CA 92556

ceo@dragonbladepublishing.com

Produced in the United States of America

First Edition April 2023

Print Edition

ARE YOU SIGNED UP FOR DRAGONBLADE'S BLOG?

You'll get the latest news and information on exclusive giveaways, exclusive excerpts, coming releases, sales, free books, cover reveals and more.

Check out our complete list of authors, too!

No spam, no junk. That's a promise!

Sign Up Here

www.dragonbladepublishing.com

Dearest Reader;

Thank you for your support of a small press. At Dragonblade Publishing, we strive to bring you the highest quality Historical Romance from some of the best authors in the business. Without your support, there is no 'us', so we sincerely hope you adore these stories and find some new favorite authors along the way.

Happy Reading!

CEO, Dragonblade Publishing

Other Lyon's Den Books

Into the Lyon of Fire by Abigail Bridges
Lyon of the Highlands by Emily Royal
The Lyon's Puzzle by Sandra Sookoo
Lyon at the Altar by Lily Harlem
Captivated by the Lyon by C.H. Admirand
The Lyon's Secret by Laura Trentham

Dedication

This book is dedicated to the quiet heroes and heroines, who don't insist on being first or greatest, but who meet challenges with grace, treat other people with kindness, and give unswerving love to their friends and families.

About The Talons of a Lyon

The death of Lady Frogmore's neglectful and disloyal husband should have been a relief. But then her nasty brother-in-law seizes her three children and turns her out, telling the whole of Society that she is a crude, vulgar, and loose woman. Without allies or friends, Seraphina, Lady Frogmore, turns to Mrs. Dove Lyon, also known as the Black Widow of Whitehall for help, paying her by promising to perform an unspecified favor at a time of Mrs. Dove Lyon's choice.

Lord Lancelot Versey has always tried to be a perfect gentleman, and a gentleman honors his debts, even when an unwise wager obliges him to escort a notorious widow into Society. But Lady Frogmore is not what he expects and helping her becomes a quest worthy of the knight for whom he was named.

And then, Mrs. Dove Lyon calls in Seraphina's promise. The favor she asks might destroy all they have found together.

CHAPTER ONE

IT SEEMED TO Lord Lancelot Versey, second son of the Duke of Dellborough, that his destiny had been decided the day he was christened. After all, a man named *Lancelot* could rebel against the name and become a wild rake. Or he could go the other way and become an exemplar of the legendary man he was named for. Not fighting dragons or dressed in armor, of course. The perfect knight, updated for the nineteenth century.

Lance had spent a lifetime molding himself into the perfect gentleman.

Percy, the eldest son, was the duke-in-waiting.

Tris, the third, had been a soldier, and now lived in the country, on an estate his father had given him. He raised horses and dogs, and seldom came into Town.

And Artie, the fourth, began as the family failure, was sent off on a tour of the world, and confounded everyone's expectations by becoming a famous travel writer.

Lance had enough to do being a perfect gentleman. Not a saint. Heavens, no. An excess of virtue horrified him as much as an excess of vice. He lived on a generous allowance from his father, enjoying his mistresses (only one at a time, since he abhorred all immoderation) and the occasional aristocratic lover, playing deep but not beyond his means, drinking heavily but not enough to be drunk.

He was popular with hostesses, because he would dance with the wallflowers, flatter the elderly and behave with courtesy in every situation. He was popular with the ladies, because he was kind and treated them respectfully. He was popular with other gentlemen because he did not stand on his dignity, understood and followed the code of gentlemanly honor, and always kept his word.

Lance had reached his thirties unwed, and even the most assiduous of matchmakers had long since accepted that he intended to remain so.

His brother Percy married at nineteen, the year Lance left his elder sisters in the schoolroom and went off to Eton. Percy accepted the bride their father chose for him and had the good fortune to fall in love with her, and she with him. Percy's wife presented him with a son before Percy turned twenty, and he now had seven children, four of them boys. That first child, his heir, was now married with an infant son of his own.

His brother Tris had also married, quite recently, taking to wife the companion of a neighbor who loved animals as much as he did. Less than a year after the wedding, Tris was proud father to a little boy. And Artie had taken a bride in some far-off corner of the world and was, according to his most recent letter, expecting a child of his own.

Lance was grateful. The Dellborough heritage was safe for another generation. The diligence of his brothers and their ladies relieved him of any need to take a wife, and even the duke, his father, accepted his lack of interest in any of the maidens trotted out for his approval.

Then, in the spring of 1816, the Duke of Dellborough died. Lance travelled to Versey Abbey to join the new duke and other members of the family for the funeral, and afterward for the reading of the will.

To his astonishment and delight, Lance discovered he had inherited several minor estates and a large portfolio of investments. His days of accepting an allowance were over. Percy and Tris argued that so were his days of idleness, but that was because they did not understand exactly how hard Lance worked at being a perfect gentleman.

When he returned to London, he moved from his bachelor apartments to a small but elegant townhouse and hired a secretary to read his correspondence and remind him when he needed to consult with a steward or a banker or some other of the dozens of minions who were laboring diligently to ensure his wealth grew with very little effort from him.

Marmaduke Halifax—Hal—was the perfect secretary, handling what did not need Lance's attention and providing all the information Lance needed when he was required to make a decision. Hal even got on with Lance's valet, which was a tribute to his diplomatic skills.

Once that was all settled, Lance could continue with the life he enjoyed, starting with a week-long celebration with his friends through all of his favorite haunts. The perfect gentleman had finally achieved the perfect life.

However, he sowed the seeds of his own destruction when he made the mistake of wagering against the Black Widow of Whitehall, owner of the Lyon's Den.

He was, he must admit, a little more to the go than usual. They had been drinking for days, after all, with only occasional bouts of sleep. Most of those had been in the bed of a soiled dove at the House of Blossoms or another of the brothels they frequented, all of them being reluctant to abandon their friends in order to visit a mistress. They had also taken brief naps in the apartment or town house of one of them, while they waited for their valets to bring them fresh clothes and prepare them baths.

Yes, he was a trifle bosky, but anyone would be, after all.

The Lyon's Den was their preferred gambling establishment. Mrs. Dove Lyon, whatever her other faults, served the finest wines and had the best food in London. She also offered all the usual games, plus whatever unusual games and wagers appealed to her clients, among whom were numbered some of the finest gentlemen in London.

Dellborough—his father, not Percy—had warned Lance never to play against or make a wager with the veiled widow. Society believed she used her wins to procure husbands for disreputable females. "The rumors are true," his father insisted, "and I will not have the kind of female who pays for a husband in my family. Don't let Mrs. Dove Lyon get her talons into you."

On the fifth night of his celebration, buoyed by alcohol, Lance forgot his father's advice.

It had seemed like a sure thing at the time. His friend Lucky, whose real name was Aurelius Chance, had been winning all evening. At cards, at billiards, at dice, at a race of grasshoppers across one of the gaming tables.

When Vincent Lord Saxton challenged Lucky to a drinking game—Lucky, whose hard head was legendary—Lance accepted the wager from the woman standing next to him without even turning to see who it was.

"I wager one hundred pounds against a favor from you that Chance will pass out first," said the woman.

"Any favor that is not unbecoming to a gentleman," said Lance.

"Done," said the woman. Lance looked and saw she was veiled. Mrs. Dove Lyon, for certain. He had a moment of regret. Unnecessary, of course. Lucky was sure to win.

Even so, with his father's warning echoing in his mind, Lance added, "And not marriage." Again, she nodded.

Lucky didn't win. Four bottles later, he gently subsided onto the floor, a broad grin on his face and the bottle cradled in his arms.

"Get up, get up," chanted his supporters. The only response was a loud snore.

"I have won," said Mrs. Dove Lyon, unnecessarily, as Vincent reeled away in search of a chamber pot.

Lance searched his memory for what he had lost. One hundred pounds, was it? He would have to ask for time for his inheritance to be paid out.

Before he could ask, Mrs. Dove Lyon reminded him, "You owe me a favor, Lord Lancelot Versey. Come up to my office, and we shall record it."

A gentleman's word was his bond. Reluctant though he was, Lance followed the lady to her office, where a contract recording the bet was already waiting.

"How did you know I would agree to the bet?" Lance asked.

Mrs. Dove Lyon gave the smallest and most lady-like of shrugs. "It pays to be prepared," she said.

"A contract is unnecessary," Lance insisted. "Just tell me what favor you want, and I shall do it." He hoped it would not be anything he regretted, but at least he had qualified the bet. Indeed, when he read the contract, the clause already read that he agreed to any favor that was not unbecoming to a gentleman and that did not include marriage.

"I have not yet decided on the favor," she told him. "The contract is for your protection and mine so that, when I approach you one month or ten years from now, the terms will be as you see them here and not distorted by memory."

She signed the contract, as did Lance, and two of her employees witnessed. One month or ten years? Perhaps she would never ask. Lance went to find Vincent and his other companion, George Buckingforth. Together, they loaded Lucky into a hired coach and went back to Lance's apartment. Perhaps they'd celebrated enough.

For the next month, Lance was prepared at any moment to receive a summons from the Black Widow. However, as he settled into his new wealth and independence, his obligation settled into the back of his mind, ignored and nearly forgotten. Perhaps it would be ten years. Perhaps it would be never.

CHAPTER TWO

London, April 1817

SERAPHINA, BARONESS FROGMORE, hid behind some bushes in St. James's Park so she could spy on two little girls while they walked—marched, almost—along the gravel path beside the pond, their eyes fixed longingly on a group of less regimented children who were feeding the ducks. She could not see the baby; only the baby carriage in which he was, presumably, asleep.

Helena, the younger of the two, took a step out of line toward the forbidden activity near the pond, and the stick the stern governess was carrying crashed down in front of her erring feet. She scurried back into line.

While the governess was still nodding her smug satisfaction, Hannah, the elder, touched her sister's hand then whipped it back to her side just in time to miss another swipe with the stick.

Seraphina, trembling in her hiding place with the effort not to leap from the shrubs and wreak vengeance on the monstrous woman, was comforted to know her brother-in-law and his minions had not yet broken the girls' spirits or their love for one another.

Tears in her eyes, she watched them until they walked out of sight.

This was the fourth day she had seen them since she'd learned that they walked in St. James's Park each morning. Each day was the same. A solemn little procession, with two nursemaids in the front, then another pushing the baby carriage, then Seraphina's two black-clad daughters followed by the governess, with two footmen bringing up the rear.

Did her brother-in-law think that she would abscond with them if they were not well guarded? He was probably right, though the solicitor she had consulted had advised her to resist any such temptation.

"Until you can disprove the calumnies against your name, Lady Frogmore, any attempt to take the children will be prosecuted to the full extent of the law, and you will lose any chance of getting them back."

Which left the other option. She needed to find a way to change Society's opinion about her. As her solicitor had advised, "Your uncle has convinced people you are little better than a tavern wench, if you will excuse my bluntness, my lady. He says you are stupid, coarse, illiterate, and ill-mannered. A shopkeeper's daughter unfit to have the care of her husband's children. Anyone who meets you will see immediately that the charges are not true. Unfortunately, you have not been much in Society."

Not, in fact, at all. Her husband Henry, Baron Frogmore, had said there was no need; that she would not enjoy it anyway, that he expected her to stay at home and keep his household. Meanwhile, he went to London for the Season and Leicester for the races and Brighton to wait upon Prinnie, all the while telling the stories his brother had exaggerated to steal her children.

Henry had liked to present himself as the handsome prince who had married the beggar maid. He'd never had much acquaintance with truth, justice, kindness or even a critical look in a mirror.

Her children were gone, and Seraphina needed to return to her lodgings to finish the chores she had been assigned in lieu of rental on her room. She had saved every penny to spend retaining the solicitor, only to find that following his advice was impossible.

"Good morning, Seraphina." The speaker was a lady she had met here in the park. Moriah Henshaw was, like her, a widow. Moriah also lived on the outskirts of Society, for her family had refused to help her when she became a widow.

"Good morning, Moriah." Given the choice between starving and finding a protector, Moriah had been forced into the life of a mistress. Not anymore. She was now a wealthy woman, but was still an outcast, taking her walks when the park was quiet. She was the only person in the world, apart from Seraphina's solicitor, with whom Seraphina had been able to share her story.

"What did the solicitor say?" Moriah asked.

Seraphina shook her head, sadly. "That I must find a way to be reintroduced to Society so people can see for themselves that Marcus and Virginia are lying."

"A good idea," Moriah agreed. "No one who met you would believe their lies for one moment."

"That is what Mr. Fortescue says, but it is impossible." She squared her shoulders, but the forces against her were too strong, and they slumped again. "I have no invitations, no escort, nothing to wear, no money to pay for any of those things." She grimaced and stamped her feet. "Bother and blast!"

"And some much stronger words," Moriah agreed. "But I may have an idea. I met someone last night who helps people like us. There is a woman who helps other women who are desperate."

Seraphina's short laugh was unamused. "I am certainly desperate."

"Mrs. Dove Lyon requires payment for her services," Moriah warned, "but perhaps she will take a promise of payment. After all, from what you have told me, you will be wealthy once you are reestablished in Society and have access to your money again."

It was a chance. Between them, Moriah and Seraphina composed a note to the lady. Moriah promised to send one of her footmen to deliver it, and Seraphina left the park with a measure of hope. Perhaps the lady known as The Black Widow of Whitehall would be kind to another widow.

If she would not... Seraphina would steal the children and run, a last desperate throw of the dice. She hoped it would not come to that.

SINCE HENRY LORD Frogmore died, Seraphina had done many things that she had been raised to consider scandalous. She walked everywhere on her own, without a chaperone or even a maid to lend her consequence. She took in laundry and mending. She cleaned and cooked for a boarding house. She hid in a public park so she could spy on people. Her own children, but still...

Nothing matched visiting a notorious gambling den. When Mrs. Dove Lyon had replied to her request for a meeting naming the date and time, and The Lyon's Den as the place, she had written back asking for a more acceptable venue.

The note in return had simply repeated the date, time, and place. So be it.

It was a long walk from her boarding house, and the time was late. Seraphina scurried from shadow to shadow, her umbrella held ready to defend herself, her attention darting from place to place. She was dressed in widow's wear, since that was all she had, but the dark gown and bonnet, and the light veil, served as a camouflage. She arrived unscathed, apart from the pounding of her heart.

As instructed, she passed the main entrance and walked down the side of the building to another door. She had been told to expect the pair of women who stood there. She had not expected them to be so large and formidable. Her words died on her tongue, so she gave the nearest one Mrs. Dove Lyon's letter as evidence of her right to be there and her need for entrance.

The woman held it up to the lamp that lighted the door, nodded, and opened the door. "Wait in the hall," she said—or, rather, growled. "Someone will show you up to Mrs. Dove Lyon's office."

Seraphina straightened her back and held her head high as she passed between the pair, her heart pounding. It reminded her of the hours of posture lessons at the hands of the deportment governess that her father had employed. She had been terrified of that crabby old woman, too, but had been determined not to show it.

The tiny hidden victories over a tyrant of her past got her past the ogres on the door and into some sort of an entry hall. She took a chair in one corner, and waited, one hand up under the veil to cover the locket that was the only jewelry left to her.

It had once belonged to her mother, and contained miniatures of her children, painted by her. Fortunately, she had been wearing it the day that Marcus arrived to turn her out of the house. She could feel the shape of it through the gown. It comforted her to know that, even in this small way, her mother and children were part of this desperate effort.

Servants came and went from a door in the wall behind her, their destination or origin one of the doors at either end of the hall. A pair of ladies strolled from one of those doors to the other, elegantly dressed in rich silk, with masks covering their faces. They did not spare Seraphina a glance.

After what seemed a long wait, a woman approached her. She was not dressed as a servant, nor was her gown as fashionable as those of the ladies—guests, Seraphina supposed—who had passed through the hall earlier.

"Lady F.?" she said. "Visitor for Mrs. Dove Lyon?"

Seraphina stood. "Yes." She showed the letter again, and the woman examined it then handed it back. "Follow me, please," she said.

She led Seraphina through a circular room where ladies as beautifully gowned as the first pair were filling plates from a long table laden with food or sitting in small groups eating and drinking. Some were masked and some not. Seraphina's eyes widened as she recognized a couple of ladies she had met on the rare occasions that Henry attended a house party near his country home and deigned to take Seraphina with him.

The next room had arched windows along one side to Seraphina's left as the woman walked straight ahead. She craned her neck to see if she could discover what interested the clusters of ladies at the windows.

"This room overlooks the main gambling floor where the men play," her escort told her. "The ladies can indulge themselves in games of chance through here."

And sure enough, in the next room, at tables of all sizes, fashionably dressed ladies were playing cards, throwing dice, and more. Seraphina stared around her, feeling safe behind her veil, and even safer because the occupants of the tables and those who stood and watched were all too absorbed to notice the shadow Seraphina pretended to be.

In one corner on the far side of the gaming room, her escort opened a door to a spiral staircase. Up was the only possible direction, so Seraphina climbed the stairs. She came to a landing and looked back to see if she should go further, raising her eyebrows in question before she remembered that the woman could not see her face.

The escort reached past Seraphina and opened the door to a long passage. "Seventh door on the left," she said.

Seraphina counted. At the seventh door, she paused and again looked at the woman, remembering to speak her question. "This one?"

The woman nodded. "You are to go inside and wait. Mrs. Dove Lyon will be with you shortly."

Mrs. Dove Lyon did not keep her waiting long. Seraphina stood when she entered, and curtsied. That was probably incorrect, since a baroness, even a disgraced widow, surely outranked the owner of a gambling den, but Mrs. Dove Lyon had a presence that transcended considerations of rank.

Mrs. Dove Lyon nodded briefly and took a seat behind her desk, saying nothing, but simply facing Seraphina. Studying her, Seraphina assumed. Seraphina had swept her veil back over her bonnet, but Mrs. Dove Lyon wore a thicker one that completely obscured her features.

"Lady Frogmore," she said at last. "How may I be of service?"

Seraphina took a deep, brief breath. She had prepared and practiced her speech. "If you know who I am," she said, "you know I am rumored to be a wicked wanton, and a bad wife." Moriah had said that Mrs. Dove Lyon knew everything.

Mrs. Dove Lyon inclined her head.

"The rumors are untrue," Seraphina declared. "They were spread by my husband's family, who want to keep me from my children."

Mrs. Dove Lyon said nothing.

Seraphina continued. "I know few people in Society and few of them know me. I come from a merchant family and my husband kept me at home. The Frogmores want me out of my children's lives because they wish to control the fortune my father left to my children, and my son's estates—estates saved by the fortune I brought into the marriage as my dowry."

She had another fear. Only the person of that son, born after Henry's death, stood between Marcus Frogmore and the title. But surely, he was not such a monster as to kill his own nephew?

She would not mention that to Mrs. Dove Lyon lest the woman think her crazed.

"Marcus Frogmore took a case to court to gain custody of the children. I knew nothing about it until after the case was decided. I have sought another hearing, but my solicitor says that, as things stand, I cannot hope to win without the support of some of those in the ton who can then stand as character witnesses. To do that, I need to move among them, to allow them to get to know me."

Mrs. Dove Lyon spoke. "So, you want me to find you a husband."

Seraphina spoke with all the horror she felt. "Dear Heavens! No! Never again."

Mrs. Dove Lyon stilled. Without seeing her face, Seraphina could not be sure, but she thought the Black Widow was surprised.

Her voice had no inflexion, though, when she said, "No." Then, "I see. Or, rather, I do not see. I can understand why a widow would not wish to marry again, but I do not understand what you want from me."

Seraphina leaned forward in her eagerness to explain. She had thought long and hard about this. "An escort, ma'am. And not just any escort, but a gentleman with an impeccable reputation in Society. On the arm of such a man, and with him to provide the invitations, I will have a fair opportunity to make my character known. If I can meet the Frogmores on an equal footing, my solicitor believes they will have no choice but to follow the terms of the will and let me have my children."

"Hmmm," the Black Widow said. "I see." She paused, her brow creased and her eyes narrowed. After a moment, she nodded. "It may work, and I know the right gentleman for the task. Let us talk about payment, Lady Frogmore."

As Moriah had warned. Seraphina flushed. "I have been denied access to my widow's stipend and to the money my father left in trust for me. I can pay you whatever you wish, Mrs. Dove Lyon, once I win my case against the Frogmores."

Talking to a veil was awkward. Seraphina had no idea what Mrs. Dove Lyon thought of her proposition. The lady said nothing for what seemed like a long time. Seraphina did not break the silence, certain that pleading would not help. Either Mrs. Dove Lyon would agree, or she would not.

At last, Mrs. Dove Lyon spoke. "No," she said.

Seraphina's heart dropped, but she rose from her chair, squeezing out a polite farewell through her dry throat. "Thank you. I will take up no more of your time."

"Sit," said the Black Widow. "I will help you, and I will accept deferred payment, but not in money."

Seraphina sank back into the chair. "What do you mean?" she asked.

"You will promise me a favor of my choosing at a time of my choosing." Mrs. Dove Lyon leaned forward in her chair. "I shall have a contract drawn up, Lady Frogmore. Read it carefully. If you choose to sign it, I shall arrange for a gentleman to escort you to Society affairs— a perfect gentleman for your purposes. In return, you shall promise to perform a task for me when I ask it of you."

Seraphina frowned as she thought. "Let the contract say that I shall perform any task you ask, provided it does not require me to do anything against the law or against morals," she proposed. Even so, it was a risk. But not as bad a risk as doing nothing.

Mrs. Dove Lyon tipped her head to one side again, the veil turned firmly toward Seraphina. When she spoke, her voice was warmer, as if she smiled under the veil. "You are not the demure cypher you would like to appear, are you, Lady Frogmore? Conditions accepted. The contract will include those provisions."

CHAPTER THREE

L ANCE HAD NEARLY forgotten his foolish wager when the summons from the Lyon's Den arrived. It had, after all, been eight months.

Eight glorious months. He had been thoroughly enjoying the life of a wealthy gentleman. He had followed the Season from London to Brighton. Not to Bath or Cheltenham. No one fashionable went to either place anymore.

He attended house parties, some decorous, some less so. He even hosted a gathering, for gentlemen only, at the single one of his estates that had not been rented to increase his income. Hal, his secretary, did most of the organization, of course, and Lance increased Hal's already princely salary, because the man deserved it.

The party was decidedly not decorous, but he and his friends took care not to flaunt their riotous behavior in front of the neighbors nor to offend the servants, so all went well. A perfect gentleman, after all, knew how to keep his peccadillos from annoying other people.

Now the London Season was in full swing again. Lance's second eldest niece was out of mourning for her grandfather and back on the marriage mart for her second Season. Uncle Lance was happy to relieve some of Percy's burden by escorting her and the duchess when

Percy was not available.

He loved the Season, and everything about it. Paying frivolous court to married beauties who took his compliments no more seriously than he did himself, conversing decorously with maidens who thrilled to his more circumspect indications of admiration, dancing with wallflowers who repaid his attention with blushing gratitude.

And, once out of sight of his charges and of the more censorious of the matrons, wagering and drinking with his friends and pursuing game pullets with pretty words and even prettier money. And rejoicing in their capture. For the night. He had become bored with his most recent mistress and had not yet met a female to replace her. Somehow, all of them began to seem insipid as soon as the excitement of the chase and the glory of the victory were over.

To be honest, even his other activities were beginning to pall. Perhaps he was sickening for something.

The night that realization dawned on him, he chased it away by drinking heavily. Buck had inherited his father's title and turned sober. Lucky had returned to his battalion in Ireland. But Vincent was happy to join him in attempting to drain half of London dry.

Waking up to a headache was neither unusual nor alarming. Waking up to a message from Mrs. Dove Lyon, however, was both.

His valet, who had helped to pour him into bed last night, had a hangover remedy ready. Lance held his nose and tipped it down and followed that with a sip of hot black coffee. A second sip had him ready to open the missive. No point in putting it off.

It was short and to the point. *I am ready to claim the favor you owe. Attend me at The Lyon's Den at two this afternoon.* It was unsigned.

Lance sighed. He would need to cry off from driving his niece in the park, but this was a prior obligation, and a gentleman never welched on his gambling debts. What on earth would the widow require of him?

At least he had been sober enough and careful enough to qualify the contract!

HIS TREPIDATION GREW between reading the summons and arriving at the Lyon's Den. His restrictions on the favor she might ask no longer seemed sufficient. What if she wanted him to give up drinking or gambling? What if she asked him to commit some act in public that would be neither immoral nor illegal, but merely embarrassing? What if she demanded an introduction to Percy or, worse, to Percy's wife, the duchess?

After he arrived and was shown to a little private sitting room, he was left for another twenty minutes with nothing to do but fret.

Ridiculous. He was Lance Versey, known throughout the ton for his address and his equanimity. Whatever it was, he would do it, and then this shameful episode would be behind him, leaving him only with the lesson not to wager anything he couldn't afford to pay.

He didn't hear her enter the room, and her voice behind him made him start to his feet. He turned to greet her.

"I beg your pardon for keeping you waiting, Lord Lancelot. An issue in the kitchen."

He bowed to disguise the fact that surprise rather than manners had jerked him upright. "Not at all, Mrs. Dove Lyon."

Even in this private interview, she had not removed the heavy veil behind which she hid her face and hair. From what he knew of how long she had been married and how long widowed, he thought she must be in her middle years, so perhaps she hid wrinkles or grey hair. She certainly didn't hide her excellent figure. The elegant evening dress in her signature black did not flaunt it, but the superb cut did it justice.

She took the seat behind the desk and gestured for him to resume his seat.

"Tea?" she asked, as a maid scurried in with a tray. "Or something stronger? I have an excellent brandy."

"The Lyon's Den is known for the excellence of its beverages," he acknowledged, wishing she would just get to the point.

She conceded the point with an inclination of her head. "Among other things. A brandy, then?"

"Yes, please," he said. How could he hurry her up?

He couldn't apparently. She poured his brandy and her tea, passed the plate of biscuits, and commented on the weather. It was hard to tell through the veil, but he was prepared to swear that she was teasing him, drawing out the meeting to see him squirm.

When he could stand it no longer, he said, "Is this merely a social call, ma'am, or do you have a favor to ask me?"

Was that too abrupt? Lance prided himself on never being rude.

"Yes, that is correct," said Mrs. Dove Lyon. Nothing in her voice or her posture suggested that she was annoyed at his introduction of the subject. He relaxed a little, until she spoke again. "I wish you to assist Lady Frogmore to prove to Society that the rumors about her are untrue."

Lady Frogmore? The one they called the Frog Princess? He had never met the female, but he had heard what was said about her.

"Are they untrue?" he asked. The claims were made by her own deceased husband's nearest relatives. Why would they claim that their sister-in-law was wanton, coarse, and stupid if she was not? Certainly, Frogmore had never brought her to London or invited guests to meet his wife in whatever God-forsaken part of the country he had his estate.

Added to that, she was a shopkeeper's daughter, or some such.

"You will need to decide that for yourself, Lord Lancelot. I do not for a moment imagine you will take my word for it. However, you pride yourself on being a gentleman. I trust you to listen to the lady, examine the evidence, and be fair and just." She nodded at him. "If you believe Lady Frogmore is telling the truth, you will escort her into Society and introduce her to your brother the duke and his wife, and to others who will be valuable in her campaign to be accepted."

"And if not?" he asked.

"Either way, our account is settled." She stood and handed him a card. "This is the lady's address. She is not able to receive visitors there, but a note will find her. Please arrange to see her as soon as possible."

Lance took the card. He knew Pond Street. It was respectable, though not a place he would have expected to find a baroness. He looked more closely. A room number. "She lives in a rooming house?" he guessed. *How peculiar.* Frogmore had been known to be a wealthy man. Lance frowned. In fact, the way Lance remembered it, the family had been in dire straits ten years ago, and that had changed when the baron married Lady Frogmore. She had brought the money into the marriage. Not a mere shopkeeper's daughter, then.

Mrs. Dove Lyon was not giving him any more information. "She will be able to tell you more. My doorkeeper will show you out."

Lance bowed again. Very well. He would meet with Lady Frogmore, and then they would see.

CHAPTER FOUR

T HE LANDLADY CLIMBED all six flights of stairs to bring Seraphina the note that had been delivered. "By a footman in livery, Lady Frogmore, would you believe."

"Thank you, Mrs. Waters," Seraphina said, taking the missive from her. She could see at a glance that the seal had not been disturbed. It wasn't a seal that she knew—a knight's helm, with something behind. Was that a lily?

"It must be important, I said to myself," the landlady explained. "I'll take it straight up to Lady Frogmore, I said. I hope nothing is wrong, Lady Frogmore?"

She waited, expectantly.

Seraphina said, "Was there something else, Mrs. Waters?"

The landlady asked, "Aren't you going to open it, my lady?"

In front of you? No, I am not. Seraphina pasted on her social smile. "I will, shortly. Thank you for bringing it up. I won't keep you from your work."

Mrs. Waters' face drooped. "Right then. Yes." Reluctantly, she retreated from the doorway, and Seraphina closed the door.

She cracked the seal that held the paper together and opened the note.

Dear Lady F.

As an attempt to disguise her identity, it failed of its chief purpose, since her full title was written, with her address, on the outside of the letter.

> *A mutual acquaintance has proposed that I make myself available to escort you. I suggest we meet to discuss the details of the arrangement. Please suggest a place and time. Your message can reach me at the address on this note.*

Suitably vague. He had signed it, simply, Lord L. V.

Who on earth was Lord L. V.?

And where could they meet?

After thinking it over, she decided on St. James's Park. She could watch her children on their daily walk, then have the discussion with Lord V.

Did he know her? For she had no idea who he was. In the end, feeling a little like a spy or an agitator in one of those Gothic novels that Henry had forbidden her to read, she wrote back with the time and place, and suggested that they both wear a white flower on their left lapel.

That should be sufficiently common as to be unremarkable, but not so common in a small circumference around her favorite watching place to have her accosting quite the wrong gentleman.

SHE WAS ALWAYS nervous when she came to the park, lest she be seen and deprived of the one great joy of her days. Today, it was worse than usual.

What if the children were running late? What if some unforeseen circumstance had them arrive after she had left concealment to meet the gentleman? What if the gentleman did not come? What if, once he had heard her out, he refused to help her? What if, even worse, he told the Frogmores what she was attempting?

She arrived fifteen minutes before the children's usual time, and it was, as always, a very long fifteen minutes. But the agony of waiting was worth it when she saw the procession coming: two nursery maids, another with the baby carriage, the two little girls walking sedately side by side, the governess, her watch in hand, nodding in satisfaction at their punctuality, and two footmen bringing up the rear.

Her daughters. Their faces prim above their starched aprons, their eyes sad. Their hands, though, twitched as if they were desperate to touch, and their bodies leaned ever so slightly together. Thank God above that they had each other.

She yearned to see her son, but she had not caught a single glimpse of him since he was five months old. Not since Marcus Frogmore and his wife and servants had moved into Frogmore Hall four months ago, just after she came out of deep mourning. Moved in to seize the children and turn her out with nothing but a single packed bag.

Help me, Lord, she prayed. *Help me turn this about. Help me win my children back.*

All too quickly, they had done their usual circuit. She watched them out of sight, emerging from the bushes once they were far enough away that none of the party would be able to recognize her if they happened to look back.

They didn't.

It was only as the little party went around a curve and out of view that she noticed the gentleman. He stood fifteen feet away on the path, and he was watching her. Had, perhaps, been watching her since she clambered out of concealment.

He was tall and fair, beautifully dressed in what passed as casual day attire among the elite, and undeniably handsome.

And he wore a white rose on the lapel of his coat.

Seraphina could feel the color rise in her face. What must he think of her? His expression showed nothing but the kind of aloof disinterest that upper-class gentlemen must practice in the schoolroom. Henry had been an expert at it, hiding everything from contempt to affection behind a facade of indifference.

Once again, she wished Henry had lived long enough to know she had given him a son. Perhaps, then, he would have been pleased with her.

The gentleman remained on the path, staring at her. Very well. She would go to him. She had tossed her veil back over her bonnet to see her darlings clearly, and had planned to replace it before the meeting, but he had already seen her face. She left the veil where it was and closed the distance between them. "Lord L. V.?" she asked.

LANCE WAS EARLY. He hoped it would give him an advantage of some kind to be here when the notorious baroness arrived. It was only when the solemn little schoolroom party had passed him that he noticed the dark shadow in the bushes.

For a moment, his mind had teemed with thoughts of kidnappers and thieves, but then a woman in widow's weeds had stepped from the bushes to stare longingly after the retreating children and their servants.

Surely it was no coincidence that the two little girls were also in black? Then he saw the splash of white on the woman's chest. He knew who she must be. She did not look coarse or vulgar, although all he could really see was her face, a sweet oval of a face with large brown eyes and a delicately molded nose, mouth, and chin.

He had not expected to have any sympathy for her after the rumors he had heard, but the longing on her face as she watched the girls march meekly away spoke to something within him. Perhaps Frogmore was correct to refuse to allow the woman to raise her children, but this scene went beyond that.

Surely, nothing she had done was bad enough to justify forcing her to hide in a bush so she could watch the two daughters she loved walk by? Having seen her face, he could not doubt that she loved them, and the unseen baby in the baby carriage. A little boy, or so he understood. The current Lord Frogmore, born a month after the death of his father.

If for no other reason than the comfort of the children, the mother should be allowed at least supervised meetings.

He walked toward her. His first impression of her delicacy was confirmed when he towered over her by nearly a foot. "Allow me to introduce myself," he said, with a shallow bow. "I am Lancelot Versey."

She blinked away the tears that were standing in her eyes, composing her expression into a blank, and curtseyed in return. "Lord Versey, I am Seraphina Frogmore."

"Lord Lancelot," he corrected. Had she never heard of him? "I am the second son of the Duke of Dellborough."

"I beg your pardon," she responded, without any of the admiring looks he was accustomed to receiving. "I did not realize. Lord Lancelot, then. Thank you for coming to meet me."

He bowed again, considering that it might be ungracious to say he had not been given a choice.

He supposed he should ask what she wanted of him. "Were those your daughters?" he blurted.

She glanced along the path where the girls had recently walked. "My two little darlings," she confirmed, a smile transforming her face. "Hannah and Helena. Hannah is the eldest, and very responsible." The smile faded and her eyes clouded with worry. "Helena is a good girl, but full of life. I fear for her, Lord Lancelot. For them both, and for their little brother, who is in the baby carriage. That governess…" She shuddered.

Lance raised his brows. "Is she so awful? Governesses must sometimes be stern to teach the children in their charge."

"Perhaps." Her one word dripped with doubt. "But it is not her stern countenance that concerns me. It is the fact that she allows no play time, insists on lady-like behavior every minute of the day, hits the children's hands with a ruler if they disobey or fidget or fail in any particular, and is doing her best to crush any joy out of them." She was marching back and forth by the time she had finished this diatribe, her hands clenched into fists.

Lance was feeling an unwelcome surge of sympathy for the little girls, and for their mother. Who was, he had to remind himself, a disgraced woman and a merchant's daughter.

"I do not see how this concerns me," he said.

Lady Frogmore examined his face, searching for something she clearly did not find. "Thank you for coming, Lord Lancelot. I shall let Mrs. Dove Lyon know you are unsuitable." She turned to walk away.

"What?" No one had ever called Lance unsuitable in his life. "But…" The woman was walking away. "Wait!"

She stopped but did not turn back. Lance hurried to catch up and stepped around in front of her.

"You require an escort to Society events, Mrs. Dove Lyon told me. I can do that."

Lady Frogmore looked up at him, frowning. "No," she said. "I do not believe you can help me, my lord. You have clearly heard the lies that Marcus Frogmore has been spreading about me and taken them for truth. You made up your mind before you met me. My escort could not possibly convince Society to accept me when he rejects me himself. Besides, I cannot let my children's future depend on someone who thinks the abuse of children—any children—does not concern him."

Ouch. "That's not what I meant," he protested. "I just..." He stopped himself before he told her that he didn't believe her claims that the governess was abusive. After all, that was her other accusation. That he had judged her on the basis of the Frogmores' opinion of her. No. Not even that, but on the basis of what rumor presented as that opinion.

As soon as he saw her watching the two little girls and had guessed their relationship, he had known the rumors were wrong about her being a neglectful mother who didn't care about her children.

Then he had met her. Nothing about her was vulgar, coarse, grasping. If those were lies, perhaps all the rest were.

And, she was correct. Lance levelled against himself the worst accusation he could imagine. He had not behaved like a gentleman. There was only one thing for it.

"I am sincerely sorry, my lady. You are right to say that I pre-judged you. Will you give me another chance?"

Again, she searched his face, and he saw her response in her own, as her eyes and mouth relaxed. "You mean it."

"A gentleman acknowledges his fault," he explained. Or, at least, a perfect gentleman does. And he had been at fault. He had come to this meeting resenting Mrs. Dove Lyon's power over him, and Lady Frogmore by association.

Her mouth twisted slightly, as if she was tasting something unpleasant. "Not the gentlemen I have known," she objected.

"Then they were not really gentlemen." Lance was confident about that. *A man is what a man does,* his father the duke used to say, but even his father thought that a gentleman's misconduct to women or to servants and other lesser beings did not count against his character.

In this, Lance disagreed with his mentor. Surely the measure of character was to behave like a gentleman with all, whomever they were?

"Tell me," he coaxed. "Please. I promise to listen with an open mind."

The look she shot him was doubtful, but she linked her hand to the elbow he offered and matched her pace with his.

"I am, as you may have heard, the daughter of a successful merchant—ship owners and importers with interests in India and the Far East, the Mediterranean, and the Americas. My husband, Baron Frogmore, inherited a failing estate from an elderly cousin. He married me to set it back on its feet again."

She took a few more steps in silence, her lips pressed together and her brow creased.

Lance said nothing, though he found himself wondering how old the lady had been at the time of the wedding, and whether the match had been her choice. Frogmore was nearing sixty when he died. From what he could see of Lady Frogmore, she was no more than twenty-five, possibly younger.

He was not a good at guessing the ages of little children, but Hannah Frogmore looked to be at least seven or eight. Lance shuddered to think of an innocent girl of seventeen or eighteen with a man in his fifties, especially an entitled opinionated blowhard like Frogmore had been.

"Frogmore preferred me to live in the country," Lady Frogmore said. "Indeed, I preferred it myself. And that is the essence of the problem, Lord Lancelot. I have never been part of Society, so nobody knows anything about me, except what my husband's brother has chosen to tell them."

Lady Frogmore fell silent again, but Lance was beginning to understand the problem. The lady—and the fact she was a lady—argued that much, if not all, of what Lance had been told was untrue. The lady, having no relatives or friends in the ton, was vulnerable to any rumors her husband's family cared to spread. But if people met her, the rumors would lose their force.

Lady Frogmore confirmed his thinking. "That is why I need someone who is highly respected and beyond criticism to sponsor me into Society. I need to prove that I am not as Marcus Frogmore has painted me."

"To what end, Lady Frogmore?" Lance asked.

"To win custody of my children, my lord."

"Have you engaged a solicitor, my lady? Surely, if you have been left custody of the children, it is a matter for the courts?"

"It is my solicitor who advised me to mend my reputation by going into Society," she explained. "I have a court hearing date to challenge my brother-in-law for custody, but he says the case will not succeed if Marcus's lies go unchallenged in the court of Society's opinion."

Lance could see that. It was a sensible strategy. If the lady could engage the sympathies of the Versey family, and of others of their acquaintance, it would be much harder for Frogmore to paint her as unsuitable to raise the young baron and his sisters.

"What of your father?" he asked. Money might not speak as loudly as birth, but it could, at least, purchase the best legal advice. And a better dressmaker. Lady Frogmore's gown might be suitable for a country widow, but it was hardly of the latest fashion and it showed signs of hard wear. Come to think of it, why was she still in black? Her husband had been dead well over the six months of first mourning.

"My father died two years ago, Lord Lancelot. He left half of his fortune to my son, a quarter to be split between my daughters, and a quarter to me. All in trust, for he had a low opinion of Marcus's ability to manage it."

Lance had not expected that. "You are a wealthy woman, then." That made her exile from her children all the more mysterious. A wealthy mother was forgiven much.

Lady Frogmore shook her head. "I have a large trust fund, it is true, and the income of it would pay enough—*will* pay enough, once I can gain access to it—for me to raise my children as a baron and his sisters should be raised. But Marcus Frogmore has convinced my trustees of his lies. I am given only the barest of allowances."

Frogmore's actions were looking more and more sinister. If Lady Frogmore was to be believed, she had been deprived not only of her children but of her fortune, for no fault of her own.

The Frogmores did not move in the same circles as Lance. He had barely known poor Lady Frogmore's husband. He had met the man's brother and his wife, but had not found their company congenial, so had not spent any time in it.

A plot worthy of a horrid novel sprung full-fledged into his mind. Or was Lady Frogmore a clever adventuress intent on deceiving him for her own purposes? He could think of one reason—that she needed to prove ill intent on Frogmore's part to win custody of the children. Perhaps one could forgive a mother for lying in such a cause.

"I assume Frogmore is guardian to the children?" he said, his tone making it a question. If the deceased baron had left guardianship of the children to his brother, the courts would need a very good reason to take it away.

"By the court's order, not by Henry's will. He left custody of the children to me, and guardianship to his cousin. He never trusted his brother. But he made no provision for what should happen if his cousin died, and he did, two days after my husband. I had no idea who the guardian was. I was not allowed to be present for the reading of the will but was told about it afterwards. I did not know that Marcus had applied to the courts in Norwich for guardianship and custody, citing my supposed sins as cause, until the day he cast me out of Frogmore Hall." Her voice shook and tight with tears she added. "He did not even let me say goodbye to my children."

The picture her words cast into Lance's mind was of this delicate little lady in her worn dress, tramping a dirt road lugging a heavy bag. He gulped away a knot in his throat. *If it was true*, he reminded himself. But then he realized he didn't need to warn himself. He believed her.

She looked down at her feet, so all he could see of her was the brim of her bonnet. Then she turned her soft brown eyes up to look into his and he could read the truth of her feelings in them. "I am frightened for my son. For my daughters too, but especially for my son."

He blurted the horrid suspicion that had entered his own mind as he glimpsed the desperation in her gaze. "You fear that Frogmore will kill him?" But it couldn't be true.

She flushed, and her eyes narrowed. "You think I am crazy to say such a thing."

Lance shook his head. "No," he said, as he turned her words, her actions and what he'd heard about her character in his mind. "May I be honest with you, Lady Frogmore?"

Her eyes widened again. "I wish you would."

"I see two possibilities. One is that you are telling the truth, and Frogmore is smearing your name in order to keep you from your children and have access to their inheritance. The other, that Frogmore is telling the truth, and you are an unfit mother."

He watched her closely. If she was duplicitous, she was the best liar he had ever met, for her face seemed to show her every emotion and many of her thoughts. Hope, followed by a grimace at his reference to Marcus's lies. Indignation and fear. Then she braced herself, lifting her chin as she challenged him.

"Which do you believe, Lord Lancelot?"

"I have already caught Frogmore in several lies," Lance told her. "You are neither coarse nor vulgar. You are certainly far from stupid. You are the daughter of a wealthy merchant, not a shopkeeper. I daresay you had the same education as any lady of my acquaintance. You did not come out into Society?"

She shrugged. "My father arranged the match with Henry when I was seventeen and I was wed within the year. He said my husband would take me into Society. Which Henry did do for what remained of the Season the year I was married, but I was with child by the start of the following year."

"Exactly so," Lance said. "You are a baroness, raised and educated as a lady. That is not the picture Society has formed of you."

Hope now shone in those brown eyes like stars, and the hint of a smile trembled on the lush cupid's bow of Lady Frogmore's lips. *Which you will not be tasting,* Lance admonished himself.

"Then you will help me?" she asked.

"I will," he told her.

CHAPTER FIVE

OVER THE PAST four months, Seraphina had cried herself dry more times than she could number. When Lord Lancelot made his disdain clear, her heart had sunk into her boots and tears had threatened again. She had not had much confidence in the plan to get Mrs. Dove Lyon's support, but the loss of even her tiny hope had been devastating.

Then he apologized. Sincerely. He begged for another chance. Seraphina was utterly disarmed.

Now she was fighting back tears again. He had listened to her. He had not gone so far as saying that he believed her, but he had declared Marcus a liar. He was going to help.

"I wonder what would be the best event to start our campaign," Lord Lancelot mused. "No one will openly object to your presence if you are on my arm, but it might be best to get people used to seeing you about before we attempt one of the larger entertainments."

Seraphina was feeling a little dizzy and was having trouble catching her breath. The switch from despair to elation was so sudden. She had thought perhaps he would take her on a walk in the park, an outing to the theater, that sort of thing. She ventured to say so. "I do not expect an invitation to a ball or a dinner."

Lord Lancelot waved her remark away. "Such entertainments will be ideal for your purpose, Lady Frogmore, but we will need to build up to them. I am thinking, perhaps the theater as a start. I will make up a party, or we will give the opposite impression from the one we intend. Do you enjoy the theater, my lady?"

Seraphina had no idea. "I have never been," she said.

He looked at her doubtfully. His words made it clear that he was not questioning her veracity, but rather, her wardrobe. "Do you have something to wear that..." Words to describe her current attire apparently failed him.

Seraphina provided them. "Something to wear that is not black, worn, and years out of date?" She sighed. So much for Lord Lancelot's help. Of course, he could not take her out looking like a bedraggled crow. "I am afraid not. It won't work then, will it?"

Marcus had refused to allow her to take any clothing except her widow's weeds. Not that it would have sufficed, even if she had brought every gown she owned. Henry had been certain a wife who lived year around in the country did not require a dress allowance or an account at even a local dressmaker, so every purchase she made had been preceded by an interrogation on why the gowns she had would not suffice.

Lord Lancelot was contemplating the trees overhead, looking pensive. "We shall contrive," he said. "I could open an account for you with a modiste."

He sounded doubtful, and rightly so. If the ton heard of such an arrangement, it would confirm everything they believed about Seraphina.

"Lord Lancelot, I cannot accept clothing from a gentleman."

"No, of course not," he said. "What was I thinking? However, I am sure we can come up with a way... I wonder..." he creased his brow so that his eyebrows narrowed together above his blue-grey eyes. His brow flattened as he appeared to come to a decision. "Yes. That might answer. My lady, what are you doing for the next two hours?"

Seraphina frowned in her turn. "What do you have in mind, my lord?"

Lord Lancelot stopped walking, turned to face her, and gifted her with a beatific smile. "I would like you to meet my sister," he told her.

But would Lord Lancelot's sister want to meet Seraphina?

He saw her reluctance. "You need allies in your fight," he pointed out. "Come along, Lady Frogmore. Where is the courage that had you risk the Lyon's talons, and meet a strange man in the park?"

Gone. With the emotional turmoil of the last half hour, she had no courage left.

Lord Lancelot's smile was kind. "Come with me, Lady Frogmore. I hate to say it, but it seems to me you have nothing to lose and the children you love to gain."

When he put it like that, Seraphina had no choice. "You are right my lord. I will come and meet your sister."

LORD LANCELOT THOUGHT about hiring a hackney, but traveling in a closed carriage with Lady Frogmore would also draw censure down on the lady. This business of being her champion was going to require a lot of thought and care!

Elaine's townhouse was no more than ten minutes' walk, though, and Lady Frogmore declared herself up to the task. Come to think of it, if she was so poor that she had to rent a room in a boarding house in Pond Street, she probably had to walk all the time.

It was unjust! A lady of her quality should not be forced to live in a lowly boarding house, wear garments his sisters would not deign to give to a charity stall and walk through the dirty streets whenever she needed to go anywhere.

And yes, in their thirty-minute conversation, his feelings had undergone a complete reversal. He was burning to right her wrongs and restore her to her proper place as a baroness *and* as a mother.

And a wealthy woman!

A thought occurred to him. Her wealth came from her father. What of her son? "May I ask an impertinent question? How much did Frogmore, your husband, leave your son?"

Lady Frogmore frowned. "Some personal possessions. Henry was not good with money, my lord. He went through it like water. The properties—two country estates and the London townhouse—were not entailed. They were heavily mortgaged. As part of the marriage settlements, my father paid the mortgages, and then made him sign them over in trust to his first-born son, or failing them, his daughters, or me, if we had no children."

She sighed, clearly deep in the past. "He put in good stewards and allowed Henry to maintain the fiction that he was in charge, but in truth, the stewards still run the estates."

Lance raised his eyebrows. It was an unusual arrangement. Clearly, Lady Frogmore's father had his son-in-law's measure. All the more reason that he should not have promoted the marriage. Still, Lance had only asked in the hopes he could set the lady's mind at rest, and he could.

"I believe that we do not need to fear Frogmore will deliberately harm the children," he said. "He will lose the estates and the income from their trust funds if anything happens to them."

She dropped his arm, and he turned to face her. She stood still in the street and stared at him, her mouth agape for a moment before a slow smile crossed her face. Her eyes shone and she pressed a hand to her heart. "I did not think of that."

Her sigh of relief seemed to take all the starch out of her knees, because she sagged slightly, and he caught her before she could fall, and tucked her hand back into his arm, supporting her as they walked, saying nothing as she recovered her equilibrium.

He measured his steps to hers, surprisingly conscious of the touch of her gloved hand in the crook of his arm. He could not understand why he thrilled to the entirely appropriate touch. Him. Lance Versey. Reacting like a fresh-faced boy who had just noticed girls had interesting curves.

It was probably because he had determined to be her knight errant. That was it. This was a natural reaction—not to the lady, but to the quest.

She tripped along beside him in her ugly but no doubt sensible half-boots, and turned her face up to his, like a flower on its stem turning up toward the sky. *No. Not a flower.* Lance didn't think that kind of poetic garbage. *Pretty face. That was it.* She said something. He replayed it in his mind. "Tell me about your sister, please, my lord."

"You'll like Elaine," he assured her. "She's my youngest sister. She's a good sort, is Elaine." Seven years younger than Lance, they had come to know one another well in the decade since she'd married and began to spend every Season in London.

Lady Frogmore said nothing, but her face hinted that she expected more.

"She has four children," he said, "and I think they must be similar in age to yours. The eldest has eight years, and the youngest is still a baby." What else might she like to know? "Her husband is Viscount Barker," he added.

He was certain Elaine would help. She had a kind heart.

However, when the butler showed him and his guest into Elaine's parlor, and he presented Lady Frogmore to her, Elaine was not as welcoming as he had hoped. In fact, she was downright cold, and very quickly made an excuse to draw him to one side.

"Lance! Whatever are you thinking bringing your paramour into my house?" she whispered.

Lance was shocked. "As if I would! That, Elaine, is exactly what poor Lady Frogmore is up against. Her brother-in-law has been spreading lies about her."

Elaine sneered. "I suppose that is what she told you."

"Lord Lancelot, I should go. Your sister does not want me here." They had not been speaking quietly enough. Lady Frogmore had turned white, and even looked a little green about the lips. She swayed where she stood, and Lance hurried to take her arm.

"You need to sit down," he told her. "When did you last eat?"

She blinked a couple of times and then shook her head, as he lowered her into the nearest chair. "Last night?" It was a question, not a statement, as if she could not remember.

"Is she sick, Lance?" Elaine asked, concern taking the chill from her voice.

"Sit still for a moment," Lance ordered Lady Frogmore. He took his sister by the elbow and conducted her to the window. "She is living in one room in a shabby boarding house. I doubt she has the money for enough food. She has already admitted to me that she is wearing the mourning clothes she had made when her mother-in-law died, because that is all that Marcus Frogmore allowed her to take with her, and she cannot afford anything else." Elaine's eyes were wide, but her glance at Lady Frogmore was doubtful.

"Her husband left her with custody of the children, but Frogmore has taken them from her, and is refusing to allow her to see them. Elaine, I believe her. And if you talk to her for a minute, you will see that she is not at all as the rumors portray her. Will you not at least order her a cup of tea and perhaps something to eat?"

Elaine did not look happy about it, but she spoke to the footman who appeared in response to the bell, then sat down in the chair next to Lady Frogmore's.

The lady had been sitting with her head on the back of the chair and her eyes shut, but she opened them when Elaine asked. "How old are your children, Lady Frogmore?"

She smiled and her eyes lit up. "Hannah is seven, my lady, and such a good girl. So responsible. Helena is the next in age and has just turned five." Tears started in her eyes but she blinked them away. "I sent her a book for her birthday. She loves books and can even read simple words. I hope she was allowed to have it."

Elaine's voice was softer as she responded. "She sounds very clever."

Lady Frogmore seemed to be looking into a beatific vision. "I think she is. Harry is just nine months old. He was five months of age, and I was just starting to wean him when…" She trailed off and turned her head away from Elaine as her mouth worked and tears began to slip silently down her cheeks.

Elaine cast Lance a look that called for help, and he crossed the room to kneel beside Lady Frogmore and offer her his handkerchief. "We will succeed. You will have your children again, Lady Frogmore. I have promised you my help, and I mean it."

"You had better both sit down and tell me all about it," said Elaine. "Lady Frogmore, I apologize for not listening to your story before I spoke. If Lance believes in you, the least I can do is give you a hearing."

LADY BARKER DID not just look like Lord Lancelot—tall and slender, with fair hair and the same blue-grey eyes—she reacted like him, too. First contempt, then contrition.

Seraphina repeated her history, expecting Lady Barker to argue as her brother had. Lady Barker, however, had a different perspective.

"I see how it was," she said. "Your husband had no confidence in his own charms, and rightly so, for he was a fat old toad. So, he kept you in the country, and told people you were plain, poor, and a peasant, lest some younger, more appealing man might steal you away."

Seraphina felt her jaw drop. That couldn't be true. Could it? Surely Henry had not had such a poor opinion of her morals. "But… But he was my husband, Lady Barker. I would never have done such a thing."

Lady Barker waved off her objection. "Of course not," she agreed. "However, men are not quite reasonable when they are jealous. And I daresay he did not trouble to know you, Lady Frogmore." She furrowed her brow, thoughtfully. "Indeed, many ladies do take lovers, though the most moral of them wait until they have given their lord an heir. Your son is very young, is he not?"

Seraphina nodded her agreement, but her indignation did not abate. "It seems we peasants have more respect for the importance of the marriage vows than you nobles, my lady."

Lady Barker just smiled at her, the same lazy smile, full of charm, that Lord Lancelot had turned on her a time or two. "You are undoubtedly correct, though in my defense, I should point out that I did not call you a 'peasant'. I said your husband did. You are not plain, either. In fact, if you were dressed to advantage, I think you might be quite beautiful."

Seraphina blinked at that. No one had ever suggested she had the capacity for beauty.

While she was absorbing Lady Barker's blunt assessment, Lord Lancelot added, "She is not poor, either, Elaine, except that Marcus Frogmore has convinced the trustees for her fortune to cut her allowance."

"He is a toad, too," Lady Barker decided. "So is his wife." She clapped her hands together. "We shall make Lady Frogmore fashionable, Lance. The toast of London. That will do them one in the eye."

"Elaine!" Lord Lancelot reproved. "Your language! Wherever did you hear that expression?"

"Our nephew Galahad, Lance," she retorted, "as you might easily have guessed."

"I have nothing to wear," Seraphina pointed out, suspecting that their brother-sister sniping might continue if she did not bring them back to the point.

Lord Lancelot seized on her intervention. "Yes, Elaine. That's why we came. Lady Frogmore's solicitor thinks a challenge might be successful, since Frogmore's will appointed Lady Frogmore as legal custodian to the children. However, Lady Frogmore's reputation needs to be rehabilitated first, he says. I am to take her into Society, but she will need the company of a reputable woman, and she will need suitable clothing."

Lady Barker began, "My dressmaker—" She stopped, and her brow creased into another frown as she guessed the problem. "Oh, but I suppose your trustees will not pay for new gowns. My gowns will hardly do. They would need to be completely remade." Her face cleared. "I have it! Lance, Barbara is with child again. Is it not perfect?"

Seraphina, who had no idea who Barbara was, was startled by the non sequitur, but Lady Barker turned to her to explain. "Our niece Barbara, who is our brother the duke's eldest daughter, is short but curvy, like you, Lady Frogmore. Her coloring is paler than yours, but she has a fondness for hues that are too strong for her. Such tones would be perfect for you. I feel sure she would be happy to make you a gift of the gowns that no longer fit her."

Talking to Lady Barker was a little like being buffeted by a small and friendly storm. Seraphina was not quite short of breath but felt she would be at any moment. Still, she could not allow Lady Barker to start giving away someone else's clothes. "Will she not want to wear them again after the baby is born?"

Lady Barker and Lord Lancelot starting laughing. "Barbara? The fashionable Lady Devereaux? Wear anything that is a Season out of date? If you don't take them, Lady Frogmore, they shall go to a maid, who will probably sell them at a clothing barrow for a few pennies."

Seraphina felt her chest lighten with what could only be hope. "I could pay a few pennies," she offered. "To make sure the maid does not lose by it. And I could make any adjustments necessary. I have been making my own and the children's clothes for years." Henry did not give her a clothing allowance, but he did not care when she raided the old trunks in the attic to find gowns from the last century with enough material in each one to make three or four gowns in the modern style.

Lady Barker leapt up and dropped a kiss in the air near Seraphina's cheek. "You are a dear," she exclaimed. "This is going to be so much fun."

"Elaine," Lord Lancelot warned, before Seraphina could say anything. "This is not a game. Lady Frogmore's whole life, and her children's lives, depend on us making the right impression."

Lady Barker waved off his statement. "I do understand, Lance, but we might as well enjoy setting the whole of Society on its pompous, judgmental ear while we see to justice for our friend."

Their friend! Seraphina had never actually had a friend. It was a lovely concept.

Lady Barker promised to approach her niece that very day, and suggested Seraphina return on the morrow, but as Seraphina stood to go, Lord Barker was announced. He was another tall handsome noble, but more heavyset than Lord Lancelot and dark-haired rather than fair.

Lady Barker immediately presented him to Seraphina. Lord Barker, rather than reacting with disgust, looked at her kindly. "My condolences, Lady Frogmore."

"Barker," his wife announced, "Marcus Frogmore is using lies to deprive Lady Frogmore of her children, and Lance and I are going to help her."

Lord Barker's amiable expression did not falter, though his eyebrows lifted a fraction. "Are you, indeed? How commendable, my dear."

Lady Barker shot him a suspicious glance through narrowed eyes. "You are not going to stop me, are you, Barker?"

Lord Barker didn't answer her. Instead, he turned to Seraphina. "I suspect winning your case for custody will require a good solicitor, my lady," he said, disclosing a grasp of the situation that neither Lord Lancelot nor Lady Barker had achieved without considerable explanation.

"I have one, my lord," she replied. "He has recommended I appear in Society to show that the stories about me are untrue."

Lord Barker continued to surprise her. "It is evident they are untrue," he said. He counted off a point by raising his hand and folding down one finger. "You are not, or at least should not be, poor. Your father was one of the wealthiest merchants in the kingdom, and Frogmore close to destitute, when they arranged your marriage."

He folded down a second finger. "You are not vulgar, as we can all see, and as a moment's thought would prove. You were educated at one of the finest of private ladies' seminaries, and I daresay you also had private tutors. Furthermore, I was present during your brief time in London after your marriage. Frogmore's behavior was, at times, less than gentlemanly. Yours was always perfectly ladylike. As for coarse! Hah!"

A third finger. "You are not a wanton. The very thought is ridiculous. Why, you were certainly not wanton in the bare two months you were in Society. You were, rather, far too innocent for your own good, as anyone with eyes and a memory would know for themselves. You have been at your husband's estate ever since, guarded (according to your husband himself) by servants who were loyal to him. Your solicitor is correct. No one, on meeting you, would believe the calumnies for a second."

He smiled at his wife and brother-in-law. "These two were an excellent choice as your allies, my dear. They are leaders of Society. Where they go, others will follow."

"Barker, I am touched," Lady Barker proclaimed.

Lord Barker folded down his fourth finger, "My last point. Marcus Frogmore, like his brother before he married you, was deeply in debt until four months ago, when he took custody of his brother's children, and suddenly started spending like a king—or, indeed, like the Prince Regent. If his actions and scandalmongering are not motivated by greed, I am a drunken costermonger."

He held out that hand to his wife and lifted her hand to his lips for a kiss. "Therefore, Lady Barker, I am not going to stop you. Indeed, I will help you, if I can. For a start, Lady Frogmore will need a suitable wardrobe."

"I am going to ask Barbara for the clothes she doesn't need, Barker," Lady Barker explained. "She is enceinte again."

"Excellent. Lady Frogmore will also need a respectable matron for company. I gather you are volunteering for the role, my dear?"

Lady Barker nodded. "Or one of our other sisters if I am not available," she said.

"That will work very well," Lord Barker agreed, "but for extra propriety, may I suggest Aunt Evelyn as a companion?"

Lord Lancelot groaned, which set Lord Barker's eyes dancing.

Lady Barker, though, appeared to like the thought. "Lady Frogmore, Barker's aunt is a pattern card for a lady. She was married for twenty-five years to a vicar. She is now a widow with two grown daughters. But you must not think she is unpleasant or judging, just because she always does the right thing. You know I am right, Lance, and Barker's suggestion is a very good one. Just because she scolds you about being idle, because she disapproves of fashionable gentlemen—" she brightened, smiling as she added—"indeed, she will very likely praise you for your efforts to help Lady Frogmore."

Seraphina thought she sounded to be exactly the right person to cause people to doubt Marcus Frogmore's opinions of her. "Will she agree, do you think?"

"Barker will persuade her," Lady Barker said, blithely. "Lance and I had thought of everything but Aunt Evelyn, Barker." She sounded smug.

"Did you think to ask Lady Frogmore to come and stay with us?" Lord Barker inquired.

"I could not do that," Seraphina protested.

Lord Barker's eyebrows could almost speak, she decided. On this occasion, they conveyed surprise, curiosity, and that continuing hint of amusement. "You will need a fashionable address, Lady Frogmore. Do you have a fashionable address?"

She glared at him and then was ashamed at her sudden anger. She could feel her cheeks flush as she dropped her gaze. He was only trying to help.

"No, by gum," said Lord Lancelot. "She has not. She would not want anyone to know where she has been living." He caught her look of reproach and his sister's alarm. Lord Barker just had those infernal eyebrows in an inquiring hook.

"Respectable," Lance hastened to add. "But poor. Pond Street, Barker. Not at all the place for a lady. You should stay with Elaine and Barker, Lady Frogmore."

Seraphina really wished that she could. "I could not impose…"

"Not an imposition at all," Barker said. "Elaine will love having you with us. Quite apart from her desire to see justice done, she has been fretting at being parted from our sons. Our eldest boy is at school, you see, and the other three have gone to stay with cousins for a few weeks." He dropped a light kiss on his wife's head.

Lady Barker smiled up at him, warmly. "Quite so, Barker," she agreed, adding, "Lady Frogmore, I know our cases are not the same, since my sons are perfectly happy and will be returning to me soon, but I do miss them so. I can just imagine being in your situation, and it makes me shiver." She gave an artistic shudder to prove it.

Seraphina had never seen a married couple of their class so openly affectionate. It set her heart yearning, but surely it was wrong to allow strangers to do so much for her. "I would not want to be any trouble."

Barker smiled, gently. "It will be no trouble to me. The servants do all the work." He offered Seraphina his hand. "Come, Lady Frogmore. We are resolved to win against Frogmore, are we not? Trust me. We need to do this."

A little dazed, Seraphina allowed herself to be persuaded, and Lord Lancelot offered himself as an escort to collect her belongings. "I'll just pop home and fetch a curricle. Can't take a lady in a hackney," he said.

"See?" Lord Barker said, vaguely. "You can trust Lance to know precisely how to behave in Society. Sit and have another cup of tea, Lady Frogmore, and I will have one, too, my dear Elaine, if I may."

CHAPTER SIX

L ANCE WAITED WITH Lord Barker and Lance's brother Percy. The ladies were soon to join them. He had to admit he was a little on edge. After a week in the hands of the whirlwind otherwise known as Elaine Barker, Lady Frogmore had been pronounced ready for her first real test. Lance was taking Lady Frogmore to the opera. Lance and others. From what Elaine had disclosed, his entire family was turning out to support the persecuted widow.

His sister and the other female relations she had rallied to the cause had taken over this week. He had hardly seen Lady Frogmore since the day he defied the dragon-lady at her former boarding house to carry her one bag of possessions down to his curricle, and then returned her to Elaine's.

He had taken her for a drive to St. James's Park every morning, with a chaperone because the carriage was closed. Her attention on those outings had been devoted to her children—anticipating, watching and recalling the little nursery procession.

Other than that, he had called at the townhouse several times. A courtesy, it was. Any gentleman would want to ensure the welfare of a lady he was attempting to help. It was not because he had any romantic interest in her.

She had been out shopping or visiting or some such, or if she had been at home, she had been surrounded by his sisters, his older nieces, Barker's aunt, and various other females, all talking nineteen to the dozen about gowns and shoes and hats and coiffures and gloves and a score of other things Lady Frogmore needed.

He was not annoyed at her unavailability. Of course, he wasn't. He simply regretted that he had wasted his time in calling when he had better things to do. Though oddly, none of them appealed since he had met Lady Frogmore.

He was glad that his sisters had taken up Lady Frogmore's cause with such enthusiasm. Of course, he was. It would not be becoming in a gentleman to resent having his quest wrested so thoroughly out of his hands. Besides, he knew his turn would come, and now it was here.

Lady Frogmore would be appearing tonight at the opera on Lance's arm. Though, to be sure, it was Percy's box, the army of women having decided that the cachet of being hosted by a duke would set the campaign off to a galloping start.

To top it off, Barker had overheard Marcus Frogmore boasting about having acquired a box for the Season. Tonight being the first of a new performance, the chances were good that Lady Frogmore's persecutors would be present. Lance bared his teeth in a grin. *Let the games begin.*

A stir had him looking toward the door. His niece Barbara came first, arm in arm with her sister-in-law, Jenna, countess to Percy's eldest son. Then Lance's sisters Isolde, Nineve and Elaine. Isolde was a countess, Elaine a viscountess. Nineve had married a commoner who did something shadowy for the government and was possibly even more respected in Society circles than Percy.

Next came Percy's duchess, Aurelia, who had given Lady Frogmore an audience three days ago, according to Percy, and taken to the lady immediately. She was now a stalwart volunteer for the cause.

Barker's aunt, Mrs. Worthington, was at Aurelia's side. They had been debutantes together and were lifelong friends. It figured. Two powerful matrons and matriarchs.

They and all of the other ladies had already spoken to friends and other relatives about Lady Frogmore's persecution. Marcus and Virginia Frogmore were completely outclassed and had already lost, and they had yet to realize they were under attack.

The last person through the door cleared his mind of every thought except awed admiration.

For a moment, Lance's eyes could not make sense of what he was seeing. The lady who entered the room behind the others was a stranger. Except he knew the face, the eyes. It was Lady Frogmore, but not as he had ever seen her.

Gone were the shapeless blacks that covered her from neck to toe and fingertip to fingertip and drained the color from her skin. She was clad in shades of lilac, with touches of silver. High-waisted, with a scooped neckline and tiny puffed sleeves, the gown was a darker lilac than the elbow-length gloves, but lighter than the flounces that trimmed the hem, the feathers in the lady's fashionable coiffure, or the slippers that peeped in and out of view as she moved.

He had thought when he met her that she would be pretty if properly garbed. He had been wrong. She was stunning. She was also shapely and entirely too desirable for his comfort. He hoped no-one noticed his reaction, which was not appropriate in a public setting.

"What do you think, Lance?" Elaine asked. "Isn't Seraphina love-ly?"

Lance was lost for words. He could only nod.

"Fine feathers do not a fine bird make," Lady Frogmore murmured.

"The point is not how fine we are, Lady Frogmore," Aurelia corrected, "but how successful in achieving our goals. Our clothes are a tool to help us play a part, and you do look very well. Lancelot, your arm please. Dellborough shall escort Lady Frogmore. Evelyn, sisters, daughters, we shall see you at the theater."

Percy obligingly offered Lady Frogmore his arm. Lance, following behind with Aurelia, wished he and Percy could trade places, but Percy was, after all, a duke, and when redeeming a lady from undeserved scandal, a married duke with an unblemished reputation was a more valuable currency than a second son who cultivated the image of a man about town.

In moments, they were out the door and into Percy's carriage, waiting outside at the head of a queue of his family's carriages, which would move up one by one to collect their own passengers now Percy had given his driver the nod to proceed.

The men were seated with their backs to the horses, as was polite. Lance rested his top hat on his thighs to hide the rebellion of his body and feasted his eyes on Lady Frogmore. She was quiet. A little flushed. With excitement? Or trepidation? The strain in her eyes hinted at the latter.

"All will be well, my lady," he offered. "No one will dare offer you insult when you are with my family."

Aurelia nodded, approvingly. "Quite right, Lancelot. Lady Frogmore, you shall have a pleasant and successful evening. I am quite decided."

SERAPHINA HAD NOT left Lord Barker's townhouse for a week, except for daily outings before the fashionable world was awake, to watch her children on their walk. Even those were made by carriage, since Lady Barker was anxious for her to stay out of sight.

The modiste, the shoemaker, and even the mantua maker had all come to the townhouse, presenting their samples and patterns, and appearing again for fittings.

She had met Lady Barker's sisters and her nieces, of course. Indeed, she had made more conversation in the past seven days than in her whole period of mourning. She had not seen much of Lord Lancelot, though. Lady Barker told her he was surplus to requirements but would come into his own as her escort.

Seraphina was nervous and excited in equal parts. Tonight would be the first time she had attended a fashionable entertainment in nine years, and she had never been to the opera, for Henry had not liked it. She hoped she didn't let Lady Barker and the others down. Especially the Duchess of Dellborough.

In her life as the neglected Lady Frogmore, she had not had occasion to meet anyone of such a high rank. Indeed, at most village gatherings, Seraphina was the only titled lady present, and she was only a baroness. Full mourning meant, at least according to Virginia Frogmore, staying at home and seldom venturing even into the garden, though she had ignored the garden prohibition for the sake of the children.

Since following the Frogmores and her children to London, her social interactions had been confined to polite greetings to her landlady, the other boarders, and people in the congregation at church.

When the carriage pulled up in front of the theater, and the Duke of Dellborough offered her his hand to help her down, she felt like a princess.

At least until His Grace came to a stop while he waited for another party to enter the theater, and she realized people were staring and commenting. All of those eyes! She looked around for Lord Lancelot, who was right behind her, with the duchess on his arm, and he smiled and nodded.

Reassured by his presence, she was able to smile somewhat convincingly, and step forward when the way was clear, accompanying

His Grace into the foyer and up the sweeping staircase to the gallery that gave on to the passages to the boxes.

The opera house looked like a palace. Not that Seraphina had ever been inside a palace, for Henry had not seen fit to present her before taking her to his country estate. But she imagined a palace would have wide sweeping staircases, vaulted ceilings, and wide halls, all marble and velvet and gilt and polished wood and rich carpets, and the opera house provided all of that. Even more so when they reached the Dellborough box, which was a pair of splendid rooms, the first leading to the other. The inner room had rows of comfortable chairs, and one side was open to the stage above an apron front.

The duke escorted her to a seat in the middle of the front row, and she looked out into a sea of people, many of them looking back. Seraphina shrank from all the faces. "Perhaps I could sit further back?" she suggested.

The duchess had taken the seat on her other side. "You are here to be seen, my dear," she pointed out. "Chin up. Smile. Ignore the gawkers."

From behind her, Lord Lancelot said, "You can do it, Lady Frogmore. For the children."

Yes. For the children. With that in mind, Seraphina sat up straight, lifted her chin, and if her smile was wobbly, she doubted anyone at a distance could tell. She could not, quite, ignore *the gawkers*, as the duchess called them. But Lord Lancelot's presence at her back helped her to pretend.

The duke walked around the back of the seats to sit next to his wife, and Mrs. Worthington took the chair next to Seraphina. "When the curtain opens, we shall have an excellent view of the stage, Seraphina," Mrs. Worthington said, "though I must say that the new gaslights provide everyone with a much clearer view than the candles and oil lamps they used to use."

The stage was presumably behind the large red curtain adjacent to the box. Seraphina cast a glance toward it, and was sorry she had, for, as she turned her head, she couldn't help but notice her brother-in-law and his wife glaring at her from a box opposite.

Mrs. Worthington put a hand over hers and squeezed. "Ignore them," she advised.

Lord Lancelot's voice spoke so close to her back that his breath stirred the hairs on the nape of her neck. "Today's playbill is a comic opera, *Love in a Village*. It tells the story of two young people who run away from home to avoid an arranged marriage. They take service, one as a chambermaid and one as a gardener in the same household. They meet and fall in love, of course."

"You do not intend to tell our guest the end, I hope, Lance," the duchess scolded. "And please, do not lean so close."

Seraphina turned in time to see Lord Lancelot roll his eyes as he straightened in his seat. "No, Aurelia. Yes, Aurelia."

The duchess leaned over to rap his knuckles lightly with her fan. "Enough of your cheek," she said, fondly.

All of the seats in the box were now full. The Versey family had turned out in force to support Seraphina, so the least she could do was to play her part. With renewed determination, she turned back to face the great open space of the opera house, and even managed to find some amusement when the duchess and Mrs. Worthington began to point out to her various prominent people of their acquaintance, giving each worthy a summary paragraph of description.

"In the third box from the front on the second level are the Duke and Duchess of Winshire. Second marriage for them both. Never did like the duchess's first husband. The duke married in foreign parts. Wore his first wife out having children. Ten of them, if you can believe!" said Aurelia, proud mother of seven.

"I see the Widow Paddimore in the box below them. Is that the Marquis and Marchioness of Deerhaven with her?" said Mrs. Worthington. "Yes. It is. She and Cordelia Deerhaven are great friends, Seraphina. Mrs. Paddimore married down, some would say, but then I did so myself, and thoroughly enjoyed it."

"The Chirburys have come to town early. The Earl and Countess of Chirbury, Seraphina. Second box from the front, second level. He is a very fine specimen of a man, but then all the Redepenning men are gorgeous." Aurelia lifted a pair of opera glasses to have a better look. "Mind you, handsome is as handsome does," she added.

They continued in the same manner until the orchestra began to play. After that, Seraphina was enthralled. She had seen traveling players at the occasional fair, but never anything to match the spectacle that unfolded before her. The costumes, the set, the singing, the acting. Part of her knew that the story was trite, but the rest was absorbed into the world the performers were creating.

Seraphina was wholly in sympathy with the heroine, who had been betrothed sight unseen. She had shown more spirit than Seraphina in the same circumstances, as she fled into hiding. Seraphina chuckled in delight as the fake gardener, who was also avoiding an unwanted marriage, and the counterfeit chambermaid each tried to resist their sudden attraction to one so far below them in rank. She gasped in outrage at the way the abandoned groom treated his former mistress.

The first act finished with a hiring fair, where each servant for hire sang about what he or she had to offer. When the curtain closed, Seraphina took a moment to emerge from her absorption.

The rest of the occupants of the box were gaily chattering when she sighed happily and turned, to find Lord Lancelot smiling at her. "You enjoyed it," he said.

LANCE DIDN'T KNOW when he'd enjoyed an opera more, not because of the performance but Lady Frogmore's reactions. She was so delightful, so natural, and unfeigned. As the silly tale unfolded, she'd gasped, chuckled, smiled, and even, at one point, clapped her hands together. Having seen the opera performed before, Lance was experiencing it anew, through Lady Frogmore.

His question, though, had her questioning herself. He could see the shadows return to her eyes and wished he had not spoken.

"I have never seen anything like it." The tiny movement of her shoulders hinted at a shrug she was too much the lady to allow. "I suppose you and your family are accustomed to such things."

"Too much so, perhaps," Lance said. "It would do us well to re-member what it was like to see a performance for the first time."

"Father brought me to this box when I was fifteen," Percy said. "I can remember how exciting it all was. I wanted to run away and join the players."

"I was in transports when I first came with Percy," said Aurelia. She smiled at him, fondly.

Percy smiled back. "You were entrancing. It occurred to me that marriage to you might bring more of such moments, and it has."

Mrs. Worthington took up the theme, saying, "A good perfor-mance can still hold me riveted."

Lance was pleased to see Lady Frogmore relax, just a little. Her sensitivity to the least criticism spoke to him of her marriage. Frog-more had clearly been a bully.

The box slowly emptied as most of the men and a couple of the women left.

Lady Frogmore leaned closer to Lance to speak in an undertone. "Was that the end of the opera?"

"Not at all," he assured her, feeling proud that she trusted him enough to ask. "There are two more acts to this opera and then another shorter opera after. Isolde and her husband have gone to see friends in another box, and most of the others are in the inner room, where Percy's servants have set up a supper. Would you like something? You have only to tell me whether you prefer juice or punch, and I shall bring it to you, with a selection of things to eat. Or you can come and choose for yourself."

"Choose for me," Seraphina decided. So, Lance went through to the other room, and joined the crowd around the table. He came back with two glasses of champagne in one hand and a plate of little savories and cakes, the second plate for Lady Frogmore under the first.

Aurelia and Mrs. Worthington were now sitting together, and Percy had brought a footman through from the inner room with a tray of food and drink. Lady Frogmore was watching the audience around the walls and down on the floor, a slight smile on her face.

Before Lance could take his offerings to her, a couple of visitors who were not of their party walked past him to greet Aurelia. Aurelia turned to Lady Frogmore. "May I make known to you Mr. and Mrs. Whitney, my dear?" To the Whitneys, she said, "Lady Frogmore is a dear friend of our sister, Lady Barker, and becoming a friend to us all."

Whitney's eyes widened, and he cast a worried look at his wife, and Lady Frogmore stiffened again. Lance prepared to leap in to protect her, but he wasn't needed. Mrs. Whitney announced, "Anyone who is recommended by their graces and the Verseys must be acceptable to me." Her glance at her husband hinted that the remark was for him rather than the rest of the audience. "How nice to meet you, Lady Frogmore."

Several other strangers had come to the box to greet various members of the family, and Mrs. Whitney's example set the tone when the duchess made them acquainted with Lady Frogmore.

Lady Frogmore began to relax, especially when Lance approached her and handed her one of the glasses, putting his own on the nearby side table. "Your drink, my lady, and I thought you could make your choice of these."

He whipped the second plate from under the first. He handed it to her. "Pick what you would like," he invited.

"Lance will eat the rest," Elaine teased. "He is a bottomless pit."

"Not a pleasant image," Lord Barker noted, in his lazy drawl.

It was then that a familiar and less pleasant voice shattered the convivial atmosphere.

Somehow, Marcus Frogmore had intruded on the duke's box. "Your Grace," he declaimed. "I cannot know how this female has found it possible to impose herself upon your generosity, but I must tell you that you have taken a viper to your bosom, as did my poor deceived brother."

CHAPTER SEVEN

E VERY CONVERSATION IN the box stopped as people turned to look at the newcomer.

Lance glared at Marcus, while fighting the urge to put Lady Frogmore behind him, the better to protect her. But before he could say or do anything, Aurelia spoke.

"Dellborough, do we know this person?" She lifted her opera glasses to her eyes and used them for a leisurely perusal of Frogmore, the twist of her lips and the flare of her nostrils clearly signals that she was not impressed with what she saw.

Percy replied in his Parliament voice—incisive, crisp, and projected so it could be heard throughout the opera house, as a hush spread outwards from their box and eyes turned in their direction. "This is Marcus Frogmore, the man who has stolen Lady Frogmore's innocent children through lies and deceit, and who continues to spread false and ugly rumors about her."

He sent the man a withering glare. "Be warned, Frogmore. Lady Frogmore is our friend, and you malign her at your peril."

Frogmore had turned purple and was opening and shutting his mouth like the creature whose name he bore, spluttering isolated words. "But. Wrong. Lies."

Aurelia lowered her opera glasses. "Lance, Barker, please remove this offensive person from our box. Without violence, if you please. Unless he struggles."

She put down her plate, stood, and turned her back on Marcus. Lance and Barker advanced on Frogmore while other members of the family in the box followed her example. After a moment, all the guests in the box did likewise.

"The bitch is a harlot!" Marcus shouted, to the rows of backs.

Lance and Barker reached him at that instant, one on either side, each cupping an elbow to lift the man off his feet. "Struggle, please," Lance hissed, in a whisper that reached every corner of the suddenly quiet box.

Frogmore did not struggle.

SERAPHINA WAS OVERWHELMED by the support of Lord Lancelot's family. No one had ever stood up for her. Not her mother, who inhabited Seraphina's earliest memories as a nervous invalid, seen seldom and briefly. Not the servants who'd raised Seraphina according to her father's strict instructions. And certainly not her father, who had only one use for his daughter, and that was to marry into the peerage so his descendants would have a title.

How exciting it was to watch Marcus Frogmore be defeated by the combined influence of the Verseys and by the strength of the man who had agreed to champion her. Lord Lancelot had been so angry—and all on her behalf. He had controlled his temper, of course, because he was a gentleman, but she could see that he was ready to use that strength to defend her honor.

It gave her the shivers, but in a good way. A thrilling way. Though she enjoyed the remainder of the performance, she did not sink as deeply into the story as she had with the first act, because part of her remained always conscious of Lord Lancelot behind her, watchful and protective.

He was so tall and slender, so gentlemanly, so handsome. So unlike Henry. She admired him more than any man she had ever met.

More guests thronged to the box in the next two intervals, all eager to meet Seraphina. With the Duchess of Dellborough and Mrs. Worthington at her side, and Lord Lancelot hovering, she was able to greet them with equanimity. It helped that the Frogmores had not returned to their box and were not seen for the rest of the night.

In the carriage on the way back to the Barkers, the duchess proclaimed herself well-pleased with the evening. "Lady Frogmore's side of the story will be the talk of the ton tomorrow," she predicted, and Mrs. Worthington agreed.

Seraphina had no doubt of it. She went to bed that night more hopeful than she had been since she was a girl of seventeen, before her father agreed to marry her to Henry.

DURING SERAPHINA'S WEEK of isolation while Elaine and Mrs. Worthington supervised the transformation of her wardrobe, her one outing each day had been a ride through the park in an unmarked carriage every morning, so she could see her children.

Lord Lancelot had proposed it, organized the carriage, and escorted her each day, with Mrs. Worthington or Elaine to chaperone.

On the day following the opera, Seraphina waited for Lord Lancelot in one of her new outfits, a stylish carriage dress in grey, with white cuffs and collar highlighted with mauve piping. She currently had more gowns than she had ever owned in her life, but most of them were in colors she would not wear until her one year of mourning ended in a few days. She was counting down to the moment, but meanwhile, the mauve piping added a touch of color that was perfectly appropriate for a widow in half-mourning.

Barbara, Lady Deveraux had not been the only Versey lady with clothing to give away. Word of Seraphina's need had spread through the family, and box after box arrived with a friendly note, or was delivered in person by a sister or a niece or a cousin, who insisted that the hat or gloves or gown or shoes or riding habit or cloak or other item was, "Just something old I was going to give to the housekeeper for rags," or "I liked it in the shop, but the color doesn't suit me," or "My dear husband threatens to move out if I buy one more hat without getting rid of some."

They were all far too sincere about it, and far too nice to refuse.

Seraphina was surprised to find that neither Elaine nor Mrs. Worthington were dressed for the outing. Then, when Lord Lancelot arrived in a high-perch phaeton, she understood. She was to see and be seen, and riding alone with a gentleman in an open carriage was perfectly acceptable.

She would have to be careful, however. His eyes drifted down her body before he pulled them up to her face with a clear effort, and the thrill she felt at his masculine reaction warned her that her heart was in danger. *You would be a fool, Seraphina, to give your heart to a man just because he is kind, and noble, and a hero in every regard.*

She feared it was already too late. She would have to make sure he never knew. He was doing her a favor out of the goodness of his heart, and the last thing she wished to do was repay his kindness by burdening him with that knowledge.

"A very fine carriage dress, Lady Frogmore," he told her, as he offered his arm. Her heart melted a little more.

She wore a poke bonnet that hid her face from the sides. She could see clearly to the front, though, for she went without a veil, trusting the shadow of the brim to hide her features from the Frogmore servants.

And, too, since the carriage was so high up and she was so hidden from view, Lord Lancelot guided the phaeton right alongside the nursery party, slowing the horses so she was able to look straight into the baby carriage and catch her first glimpse in four months of her baby boy.

Tears obscured her vision, but she kept blinking them away, afraid to miss even a moment.

Then it was over. The lead servant turned off onto a path and the others followed, while Lord Lancelot had to continue along the carriage way. "Are you well, Lady Frogmore?" he asked when she remained silent.

The only response Seraphina could manage was a sob. With the tears now coming thick and fast, she could not see what he thought of her breakdown, but she could feel the carriage surge forward as the horses picked up their pace. They turned a corner and went into shadow, the sun no longer beating down on her shoulders.

The team stopped, and Lord Lancelot put his arms around her. "We are private, my lady," he said. "You can weep now."

"He has grown so big," she wailed. "And it has been so long. Lance, he looked up and he did not even know me!"

CHAPTER EIGHT

FOUR SISTERS AND a succession of mistresses had taught Lance that, when a woman needs to cry, it was best to let her do so. He also knew they needed comfort rather than sensible masculine advice. Still, he could not resist telling her, "He will learn to love you again soon, my dear. Will he not take his cue from his sisters?"

She nodded at that, looking up to his face as if for reassurance. Tears continued to well in her eyes and spill down her cheeks, but the shuddering sobs had ceased. Lady Frogmore—Seraphina, perhaps, for had she not called him Lance in her turmoil?—Seraphina rarely allowed herself to display her emotions. To break down like this in front of him, she must have at least some small regard for him? Surely?

He berated himself. Here he was thinking about how he felt instead of focusing on Seraphina. He patted her back, which was a mistake, since she took it as her cue to pull away, leaving his arms.

"I am sorry," she apologized. "I know that men do not like hysterical women."

"You are the furthest possible thing from hysterical," Lance reassured her, fighting the urge to pull her back against his body and give her thoughts another direction by kissing her. "That you trust me enough to let me see you weep makes me feel very privileged."

"I *do* trust you." She sounded surprised, as if such a thing had never happened before.

"You can," he assured her, making it a vow.

"Thank you for understanding. Thank you for making it possible for me to see him."

"We shall come in the phaeton every morning, if you wish," he assured her, for he had made sure he was available to escort her each day.

He helped her wipe her tears, assured her that she looked respectable, and did not tell her that her eyes were like drowned pansies, because he would cut his tongue out rather than let such florid language escape him. They did, though. Or, rather, they didn't, since the kind of pansies he was thinking about were yellow as well as the rich soft brown he recognized in her lovely eyes, which were not at all the shape of pansies.

In fact, it was not just florid, it was stupid. Perhaps a poet could describe how beautiful her eyes were, even swimming with tears. Lance was certainly not a poet, but he knew loveliness when it stirred his heart along with less poetic physical reactions.

As they drove out from the shelter of the trees, he saw a phaeton that he knew. "There's my friend Vincent," he said. "But who is that with him?" Silly to ask Seraphina, for he had been present for every introduction to people she was likely to know.

However, when she peered in the direction he indicated, she said, "That is my friend Moriah. Oh my. That must be the man…" She clapped both hands over her mouth, as if to stop the words.

Intrigued, Lance sent his horses in the direction of the pair. "Let's go and talk to them," he said.

In moments, Lance was presenting Vincent to Seraphina. He guessed she was higher ranked than her friend, for he knew at least by name if not by sight every peeress and duke's or marquess's daughter in the ton, and he had not heard of a Moriah. Or, at least, not a respectable one. "Lady Frogmore, allow me to make known to you Lord Saxton. Vincent, Lady Frogmore has been kind enough to accept my escort into polite Society."

He gave his friend a glare, warning him against any negative remarks, but Vincent bowed as well as he could from the driver's seat of his phaeton, and asked, "Lady Frogmore, may I make you acquainted with Mrs. Henshaw?"

Moriah Henshaw! Lance had heard of the woman, a notorious mistress, though she was the granddaughter of an earl. Perhaps he should take Seraphina away. Knowing Mrs. Henshaw would not serve her well in her custody battle.

Seraphina had no such qualms. "Moriah and I are fast friends," she declared, smiling.

Vincent, with a challenge in his own eyes, said, "Mrs. Henshaw, may I make known to you Lord Lancelot Versey. Lance, I am on the same mission as you, as it is my privilege to escort Mrs. Henshaw back into her rightful place." He jutted his chin at the last few words, and Lance was ashamed of his instinctive reaction. If she was a friend of Seraphina's and had a champion in Vincent, then she was worth supporting.

"Mrs. Henshaw, any friend of Lady Frogmore's and of Lord Saxton's is a person worth knowing. It is a pleasure to meet you."

IT WAS FORTUNATE that the Frogmore children took their walk so early, for a few days later, Seraphina had a morning meeting with her trustees. Percy was going with her. Indeed, he had requested the meeting, and the trustees, who had been ignoring requests from

Seraphina and her solicitor, meekly fell into line.

Lance had to concede that Percy's dukedom made him the best person for that particular job, but he could at least take Seraphina to see her children. He did, and the germ of another idea began to grow as he saw her wistfully watching them out of sight.

He got her home in plenty of time for the trip to the solicitor. They travelled in style in the ducal coach, Seraphina escorted by the Duke of Dellborough and chaperoned by Mrs. Worthington, with Lance tagging along. Not that he expected to be of assistance, but he didn't quite trust Seraphina's safety to anyone else.

In the coach, Percy asked about the trustees. "Are they your brother-in-law's creatures, Lady Frogmore?"

She thought about it, her head on one side like a little bird. "I do not think so, Your Grace," she concluded. "They are men of my father's age. One was his solicitor, Mr. Cranshaw. The other two were friends of my husband, Viscount Penningway and Lord Matthew Tewksbury. My father believed they would know better than his own friends what the widow and children of a baron might need. All three share my husband's and father's low opinion of women, so are inclined to believe that those of my sex will misbehave unless they are kept short of money. But, since they knew Henry, they must also know that he thought even less of his brother than he did of me."

Seraphina's solicitor met them outside the building where they were meeting the three trustees at the office of Mr. Cranshaw.

The Dellborough footman went ahead of them to open doors until they arrived at their destination, to be greeted by an obsequious clerk and ushered through into the presence of the trustees. Three elderly men sat around a table, their corpulence evidencing the usual effects of a lifetime of indolence and indulgence. Lance recognized Penningway and Tewksbury, so he guessed the other must be Cranshaw.

There was only one other chair.

The three trustees stood, with some difficulty. "Duke," said

Tewksbury, in greeting, and promptly sat down again. The other two plopped down as well.

Percy managed to sound surprised when he said, "Gentlemen? There are ladies present." Lance had to give him credit; he himself would only have managed to sound annoyed.

They hoisted themselves reluctantly to their feet again.

"Have you met the gentlemen, Lady Frogmore, Mrs. Worthington?" Percy asked.

"I have, Your Grace," Seraphina said, and dipped the men a shallow curtsey.

Mrs. Worthington acknowledged the two men she knew. "Good day, Lord Penningway, Lord Matthew."

They bowed, with a creaking of corsets.

Percy turned to Seraphina. "All three gentlemen, Lady Frogmore?"

"Once, Your Grace, when I visited each of them to ask for my allowance."

Percy pursed his lips, nodded, then said. "Penningway, Tewksbury, you know my brother Lancelot, and this other gentleman is Mr. Fortescue, Lady Frogmore's solicitor." He looked at the one person in the room who had not been named.

"Cranshaw," Tewksbury mumbled.

Percy continued to play the polite introduction game while the trustees longed for their chairs. "Mrs. Worthington, may I make known to you Mr. Cranshaw. Mr. Cranshaw is, I take it, the third of the trustees charged with the care of your fortune, Lady Frogmore."

"They'll have to wait in the other room, duke," Tewksbury burst out. "No chairs. Only expected you."

Percy led Seraphina to the one remaining chair and made a show of helping her to be seated. "Mr. Fortescue, would you be so good as to poke your head out the door and tell the clerk we'll need some more chairs? Another four, if you please."

"I don't know why all these people are here," Penningway complained to Tewksbury.

"I can tell you that," Percy replied, agreeably. "Lady Frogmore is here because she has some questions for you. Mrs. Worthington has come as her chaperone. I, to insist the lady's questions are answered, my brother because I chose to bring him with me, and Lady Frogmore's solicitor to advise her in the event she requires a legal opinion. And here are the chairs. Mrs. Worthington, may I see you seated next to the baroness?"

Mrs. Worthington took the chair next to Seraphina and gave Seraphina a nod, whereupon Seraphina asked the gentlemen to be seated, which the trustees did immediately and with a sigh of relief. Everyone else sat as soon as their chair arrived, Mr. Fortescue taking the last.

Lance had to admit Percy was very good. He prompted Seraphina to begin. She asked why her allowance from the trust had been cut to a pittance—when she named the amount, Lance realized he spent more on the wages of his least scullery maid, who also received food, clothing and shelter as part of her employment.

Penningway sputtered outrage, but his words made no sense, until Percy managed to elicit the information from the three trustees that the rest of Lady Frogmore's allowance was being paid to Marcus Frogmore. "The woman abandoned her children to travel to London, so Frogmore said to cut off her funds so she would have to go home," Tewksbury explained. "He is looking after it for her."

"But she must have found herself a protector," Penningway speculated, "for look at her! Tricked out in the height of fashion. That sort of garment doesn't come cheap. Is it you, duke? Take it from an older and wiser man; that sort of woman is not worth the trouble they cause."

Lance leapt to his feet, but Percy waved him down. His voice, when he spoke, was lethally quiet. "You insult not Lady Frogmore alone, but also me, my lady wife, and Mrs. Worthington, who has been the lady's chaperone since she moved in to live with my sister Lady Barker, whom you also insult with baseless allegations."

Mr. Cranshaw appeared to be attempting to hide himself behind his little stack of papers, and even Tewksbury was a little taken aback. But Penningway attempted to be avuncular. "Now, now, duke, no need to get in a—"

Percy interrupted. "The correct form of address, Penningway, is *Your Grace*." It was true. Penningway and Tewksbury had both adopted a familiar form of address used between equals and friends. Percy's none too subtle reminder that they fitted into neither category silenced them both.

"Cranshaw," Percy barked. "What steps did you take to find out whether Marcus Frogmore was telling the truth before you began sending him the money?"

"Wh–what st–steps, Your Grace?"

"No need, du—Your Grace," Tewksbury assured him. "Word of a gentleman."

After that, Percy and Fortescue between them eviscerated the three men. Lance would have settled for a literal gutting, so angry was he at the cavalier way they had treated Seraphina, but he had to admit that the emotional and intellectual destruction he witnessed was more elegant.

Percy explained the results of his own investigation. Lance had not even been aware that he'd done one, and Seraphina's startled glance confirmed she had not known either. They listened in awed silence as Percy reported the eyewitness accounts of horrified servants and villagers who saw Lady Frogmore evicted without notice from the home owned by her son, refused even a moment to farewell her children, and forced to leave with only the clothes she could cram in one bag.

The vicar had given her refuge, but when the Frogmores headed to London, she followed them, and appealed to her trustees for the allowance left to her by her father.

Percy was building up steam. "You refused to listen to what she had to say. You took her money and gave it to a man who is such a proven blaggard and scoundrel that his own brother refused to leave him any responsibility for his children. You left Lady Frogmore so poor she had to take in mending to pay for food. She, one of the richest women in England, had to accept cast-offs from my sisters and nieces just to dress decently, and make them over herself because she could not afford a seamstress. Call yourself trustees! You have been derelict in your duties and acted in a thoroughly untrustworthy manner."

"B-b-but Marcus gave his w-word," stammered Tewksbury.

Percy enumerated just some of the expensive items that Marcus and his wife had purchased since taking charge of the children, when they began to receive the income from the children's trust as well as Seraphina's. "Since he was near penniless when his brother died, I imagine you can guess how he has paid for his new carriage, his billiards table, his French mistress, the redecoration of the ladies' parlor, a private box at the opera, and an extensive new wardrobe for himself and his wife, while his brother's children still wear black a year after their father's death."

Fortescue started mildly. "I have read the terms of the trust. I am not as experienced as you, Mr. Cranshaw, but I cannot find any clause that authorizes you to decide to withhold the interest on the trust account specified in the will as due quarterly to Lady Frogmore. Nor can I see a clause authorizing you to make a payment due to a beneficiary to a person not named in the trust deed. Can you explain to me the legal basis for your decision, sir?"

Cranshaw couldn't. Lance was beginning to enjoy the show.

Fortescue then pointed out that there was a provision in the trust documents for the trustees to appoint other trustees in their place. "That might be something you gentlemen wish to consider."

Penningway rallied, pontificating about their sacred duty to their dear, departed friend.

Percy expressed the opinion that Lady Frogmore's father was unlikely to look kindly on his provisions for his daughter being ignored. "It is my understanding, gentlemen, that malfeasance on the part of a trustee is a serious charge. I believe Lady Frogmore would be within her rights to ask her lawyer to pursue such a charge against you."

Fortescue, responding as if they had rehearsed their parts, and perhaps they had, begged him to give the gentlemen time to consider.

"What is your opinion, Lady Frogmore?" Percy asked. "Should these incompetent miscreants be allowed time to make up their minds to do the right thing?"

"Perhaps, Your Grace, they might restore my allowance while they are thinking," she suggested.

"We cannot," Tewksbury squawked. "Not until the next quarter. This quarter's payment has already gone to Marcus Frogmore."

"Either get it back—" Lance suggested, for why should Percy have all the fun—"or pay Lady Frogmore out of your own money."

Mrs. Worthington stood, bringing Percy, Lance, Fortescue, and a subdued Cranshaw to their feet. "I think we are done here," she said. "Aurelia and our other friends will be most displeased when they hear what has been going on."

Tewksbury leapt to his feet with more vigor than he had showed for the past hour. "You would ruin us? But that isn't fair!"

Mrs. Worthington simply said, "Are you ready, Lady Frogmore?"

"Please! Mrs. Worthington!" Pennington begged as he also lumbered to his feet. "Is there nothing we can do to change your mind?"

"May I make a suggestion, Your Grace?" asked Fortescue. "Perhaps you and your family would consider holding your fire if the three gentlemen immediately begin to fulfil their duties to the trust established by Lady Frogmore's father. As a first step, they could restore Lady Frogmore's income for this quarter. Within a week, perhaps, which would also give Your Grace and Lady Frogmore time to come up with a replacement list of trustees. Younger men, I would suggest. Men who will see it as their duty to support Lady Frogmore rather than assist in an attempt to ruin her."

Cranshaw whispered that the trustees were the only people empowered to choose their replacements.

"Or the Crown through the courts, if a case of malfeasance is proven against you," Fortescue reminded him, his voice gentle. "You would be wise to choose the next set of trustees from Lady Frogmore's list, or His Grace will ask the Prince Regent to do it for you."

Percy's tone was also kind. "It is time to retire, gentlemen. The alternative is social and financial ruin, and nobody would be well served by the scandal. The truth is that a plausible scoundrel persuaded you to abandon your solemn duty and instead assist him in the social and financial ruin of the very lady her father intended you to protect and serve. You must see that it is my duty to the Sovereign and to the Realm to ensure that you are removed as trustees, however that is achieved."

He said nothing more; merely offered Lady Frogmore his arm and left the room. Lance had never listened to Percy give a speech at the House of Lords, but after this performance, he knew his brother must be good at it. He offered his arm to Mrs. Worthington.

It was left for Fortescue to have the last word. "His Grace will accept your decision by tomorrow, gentlemen. A single note to his residence, signed by all three of you, will suffice. A failure to send a note will signify your refusal of His Grace's terms."

CHAPTER NINE

T HE MEETING WAS emotionally draining, but enormously satisfy-
ing. How different from her first and only visit to the trustees,
when she first came to London. She had gone to Cranshaw, first, but
he told her there was nothing he could do, and she should return to
Sussex and behave herself.

Penningway lectured her, berated her, and refused to allow her to
speak in her defense, before ordering her escorted from his townhouse.

Tewksbury had been jolly and pleasant right up to the point that
he offered to set her up under his protection. When she finally
understood what he intended, she was outraged, and said so. Tewksbury also had her escorted out.

Before she met Lord Lancelot, no one had defended Seraphina
since a beloved governess did her best, only to be dismissed for her
impertinence. And that had been more than a decade ago.

Now, a whole room full of people had taken up cudgels—or
words, at least—on her behalf.

She was grateful to each of them, of course. Mrs. Worthington had
proved a true friend. His Grace the Duke of Dellborough had used his

consequence to excellent effect and had shown wisdom and skill in handling the trustees. Mr. Fortescue's interventions had been brilliant. But none of them would have been there without Lance.

Lance—she could not help but think of him by the shortened form of his name that his sisters and brothers used—Lance was a true hero. From the moment he had taken up her cause, he had worked tirelessly to make allies of his family and friends. She was beginning to believe she would win her children back from the Frogmores, and if she did, it would be entirely due to Lance and his support.

She wanted to say as much to him, but he had the carriage drop him at his townhouse. He would be at the ball tonight, but he was not escorting her. He had asked for a dance, so perhaps she could talk to him then.

It was a benefit ball, a ticket-only, glittering event hosted by the Duchess of Winshire to raise money for one of her charities.

Yesterday had been the anniversary of Henry's death, and for the first time in a year, Seraphina was to appear in public in a color other than black, grey, white, or a pale shade of purple. She felt rather guilty about how delighted she was.

"It does not seem right," she told Mrs. Worthington, who had brought her dresser to put Seraphina's hair up. She made a face at herself in the mirror. The reflection had its hair piled in coils and curls, highlighted with bright but inexpensive pins decorated with enamel flowers in the same colors as her gown.

A warm rose, it was, with touches of a lighter pink and a rich wine. The deeply scooped bodice was even lower than the one that had shocked her when she saw herself in it on the evening of the opera. Around her neck, she wore her mother's locket. It was the only part of the reflection that felt familiar.

"What does not seem right?" Mrs. Worthington asked. "The gown is delightful on you, Lady Frogmore, and the hue is lovely."

"My daughters were still in black this morning. I made their mourning wear with wide seams and deep hems so it would last for six months, but they are still in the same garments, with extra fabric let in at the sides and attached around the hems."

"Ah." Mrs. Worthington nodded. "I understand the feeling. When my husband was bedridden before his death, I curtailed my walks and rides because he was unable to enjoy such activities. He scolded me for sloppy thinking, dear man. He pointed out that my refusing to use my legs would not make his work any better."

Seraphina saw her point. "My girls' clothing will not fit better or be less black if I go to this ball in sackcloth and ashes, you mean," she said. "You are correct, of course. I will dress them as brightly as flowers when they are in my care again."

"Focus on that, Lady Frogmore," Mrs. Worthington advised.

"Done, my lady," said Curtis, the dresser, "and very nice if I do say so myself."

"You've done well, Curtis," Mrs. Worthington agreed.

Seraphina thought so, too. "It looks so elegant, Curtis. You are very clever. Thank you."

The dresser surprised her with a smile—she was, in general, a dour person. "My pleasure, my lady."

Lord and Lady Barker also expressed their delight at her gown. "The color suits you much better than it suited Barbara," Elaine said, while Lord Barker pronounced the overall effect to be charming.

The carriage was waiting. Winshire House, the venue for the ball, was a magnificent townhouse in the oldest part of Mayfair, and the queue of carriages was enormous. During the thirty-minute wait to reach the steps, the Barkers, who had been out for the afternoon, asked about the meeting with the trustees. Mrs. Worthington had them laughing at her description of the horrid men and their reaction to Percy's championship of Seraphina.

"Mrs. Worthington was wonderful, too," Seraphina insisted. "She threatened Lord Pennington and Lord Matthew with social ruination."

"I did nothing of the sort," Mrs. Worthington insisted. "I merely told them that the duchess, the Versey ladies, and all of their friends would be most displeased with them." She tried to look stern, but her lips twitched and her eyes twinkled.

Elaine giggled.

Lord Barker leaned toward Seraphina and, in a loud stage whisper, said, "She threatened them with social ruination."

"She really did, but she didn't say so at all," Seraphina confirmed. "So clever. They all were. I am so very grateful."

"My dear," said Mrs. Worthington, "we must help you. You and your children have been treated dreadfully, and no one with any moral fiber at all could refuse to assist."

"Besides," Elaine commented, "if we had refused, Lance would just have hounded us until we changed our minds. He is meeting us at the ball, you know. I daresay he shall be most impressed with how lovely you are in that color, Seraphina."

Sure enough, Lord Lancelot was waiting on the steps of the grand house when their carriage drove in. Seraphina guessed that Elaine was right, given that his jaw dropped and his eyes widened when he saw her.

He recovered quickly and hurried down the steps to offer her one arm, and Mrs. Worthington the other. "I shall be the envy of every man here," he declared. "Two such lovely ladies on my arms! I shall probably be cashiered from my club for greed."

Mrs. Worthington rapped his arm with her fan and told him he was a cheeky boy.

They passed through the receiving line, being greeted by the duchess herself and several other ladies who were on the board of the charity for whom the ball was raising funds. The duchess greeted Mrs. Worthington and the Barkers as friends, and Lord Barker introduced Seraphina.

Around them, other conversations stopped. While the Verseys' support had won Seraphina a conditional acceptance in Society, the influence of the Duchess of Winshire was enormous. What she said next could mean total success, or abject failure.

"Lady Frogmore, I am charmed to meet you at last. I have been hearing about your sufferings, and I am so sorry I was not aware earlier. You may be certain of my support, my dear. Indeed, we are all agreed, ladies, are we not?"

The other ladies on the board nodded, and all had something pleasant to say to Seraphina as her party passed along the line.

The ballroom was enormous, magnificent, and very full. "Anyone who can afford the price of a ticket can come," Elaine told Seraphina. "Despite that, even people who generally prefer more exclusive entertainments still want to come, for the duchess is much admired. Though there are people like Percy and Aurelia who would rather give her a donation for her cause and stay home."

Seraphina recognized some of the people she had met at the opera, and others Lance or Elaine or Mrs. Worthington had pointed out to her as they passed them while out and about. Moriah was here, too, escorted by the Earl of Saxton. She sent her friend a quick smile.

To Seraphina's surprise, gentlemen took her appearance in color as an invitation to petition her for a dance. They were correct, of course. She was no longer in mourning, as the rose gown indicated. Society's rules permitted her to dance again.

She had not expected the number of supplicants. Within minutes of their arrival in the courtroom, all of her dances were claimed. Elaine was delighted. Lance, meanwhile, grumbled he was fortunate he had secured her supper dance beforehand, and he could see he would have to wake up early if he wanted to remain ahead of the scoundrels who would pursue her now that she was out in Society again.

Seraphina ignored the leap of her heart. He was talking about dancing. Wasn't he? She should not imagine anything else.

She was not, however, imagining his glower as the first dance was announced and her first partner for the evening escorted her onto the floor.

Whatever was bothering him, he was too much the gentleman to refuse to do his duty. He went to offer himself as a partner to a lady without one. She next saw him out on the floor, politely focused on a spectacled debutante who stood on his feet twice that Seraphina observed.

That could have been Seraphina, but for a conversation she had had with Elaine a couple of weeks earlier, at another ball, as she watched the dancing with her foot tapping.

"Do you enjoy dancing?" Elaine had asked.

"I used to," Seraphina told her. "I have not danced since I left school. Henry did not like me to dance with other men, and he felt himself too old to dance with me, himself."

"My goodness," Elaine commented. "We had better get you a dancing master!"

Seraphina was grateful for Elaine's foresight. Several of the dances this evening would have been completely new to her without her lessons.

As it was, she felt she acquitted herself well, though she found the first waltz of the evening awkward. Her partner of the moment seemed to have trouble focusing his eyes above the neckline of her gown, and kept trying to pull her closer to him, so that she had to reprimand him.

"Lord Thomas," she said, in a low voice and with a pleasant smile, "you will keep the proper distance or I shall make a scene immediately, and I shall explain my reasons to our hostess as well as to my chaperone, Mrs. Worthington, and to the Duchess of Dellborough."

Lord Thomas looked chagrined. He stopped his mischief, and they did not exchange another word until the dance was over, whereupon he walked off, abandoning her in the middle of the floor. He only managed a couple of strides before Lance stepped in front of him and murmured in his ear.

Lord Thomas turned, and bowed to Seraphina. "Thank you for the dance, Lady Frogmore," he croaked. He shot a glance at Lance. At Lance's nod, he sidled away, and Lance offered Seraphina his arm and the whispered words, "Nasty piece of work. He won't approach you again, Seraphina."

He returned her to Elaine's side, just in time, for the Duchess of Winshire called for everyone's attention, and handed over to someone called Lady Sutton, who spoke passionately, but briefly, about the benefits of supporting education for women of talent and intelligence who lacked families of means.

The Duchess promised, with a twinkle in her eye, that they would have opportunities to donate before the evening was over and invited them to continue to enjoy themselves.

Seraphina was awed. "Educating women so that they can support themselves with dignity," she said. "What a wonderful notion!"

Lance opened his mouth to say something, but her next partner came to claim his dance. "We can talk about it over supper," Lance said.

When the time came, Lance waltzed like he did everything else— superbly. He did nothing to discompose her. He kept the proper distance, did not ogle her breasts, or ignore her while he ogled others, did not press her hand, or make suggestive remarks.

Even so, she was definitely discomposed. Her pulse quickened. She felt heat radiating from where his hand rested on her waist—heat and tingles. The ache in her core bewildered her, though it was not unpleasant, and for some reason, her breasts felt heavy and sensitive.

She had felt these sensations before when touched by Lance, but never to this extent. *It is because I am in love with him*, she told herself. Then, with some surprise, *it is lust*. She had never felt desire for any man. Never expected to.

She would do nothing about it, of course. Even if he showed interest, she did not have the cavalier attitude to morality that many of the ton displayed, and she would certainly do nothing to give ammunition to Marcus in his war against her.

But how nice to know she was not, after all, cold by nature, as Henry had claimed.

Supper was fun. They sat with Mrs. Worthington and the Barkers, and Percy's and Aurelia's married children and their spouses, and had a vigorous discussion about the duchess's notions about educating women.

Several of the husbands decried the idea, and Seraphina was indignant until she realized they were teasing their wives. And their wives teased them back! Seraphina had never seen anything like it.

The Verseys, it seemed, had all made love matches. She said so to Lance, under cover of the other conversation, and he told her that Percy and Aurelia had fallen in love after their arranged marriage, and after that, had encouraged the rest of the family to seek love rather than the more common aristocratic goals of breeding, power, wealth, or land.

After supper, she needed the retiring room. She and Mrs. Worthington found it upstairs and at the end of a passage—two lovely rooms with comfortable chairs, screened areas for the necessities, and mirrors above tables for fixing hair or other details of appearance.

Each room was attended by a maid, who was available to sew up hems, or wash out spots, or replace hair pins.

"Such impressive organization!" Seraphina said to Mrs. Worthington.

"Eleanor Winshire is known for it," Mrs. Worthington replied.

Despite the size of the rooms and the number of facilities, there was a queue for the dressing screens. Mrs. Worthington insisted on Seraphina going first, and Seraphina conceded, since she had had a glass of champagne and two of punch in the course of the evening, and the matter was becoming urgent.

When Seraphina came out from behind the dressing screen, Mrs. Worthington was nowhere to be seen, so she must have taken her turn.

Seraphina stooped to peer into one of the mirrors and fiddled with a couple of her pins to fix a lock of hair that had fallen down. Focused as she was on the mirror, the first she knew of the presence of one of her enemies was when the woman's reflection appeared in her mirror.

Seraphina's breath caught in her throat and her chest constricted. She turned to face her. "Virginia," she said.

"You nasty, common, little bitch," her sister-in-law hissed. "How dare you come here, swanning around on the arm of your fancy man, pretending you are fit for the company of your betters."

"You insult Lord Lancelot Versey," Seraphina replied, pleased that her voice was steady, though inside she was shaking like a blancmange. "He is a perfect gentleman, and you are wrong to speak such untruths."

Virginia didn't listen, which came as no surprise. "Marcus and I will see to it that you are put back in the gutter where you belong, and I can promise you that you will *never* see your children again."

Mrs. Worthington had emerged and stood behind Virginia. "I have a promise for you, Virginia Frogmore." When she spoke, the woman started, and twisted to see who was there.

"You and your husband," Mrs. Worthington continued, "have lied and cheated to see Lady Frogmore deprived of her place, her fortune, and her children. I promise you that your sins have been uncovered, and you will not be allowed to enjoy the fruits of your lies and deception. Now go home before I tell Her Grace of Winshire that you have been threatening another of her guests."

"You cannot support her!" Virginia whined. "She is not one of us!"

"*You* are not one of us, Mrs. Frogmore," Mrs. Worthington declared. "Ladies do not spread false gossip. They do not cheat widows out of their income. Lady Frogmore has powerful allies. If you are wise, you and your husband will return the children and retire to some place you can afford without stealing from the little baron. I believe Italy might be suitable."

Two other women had entered the room while Mrs. Worthington was speaking and were listening avidly. Virginia must have noticed, because she suddenly put both hands over her face and rushed from the room.

The starch went out of Seraphina's knees and she sank onto the stool in front of the mirror. Her breath, as she released it, was ragged. Mrs. Worthington sat beside her and put an arm around her shoulders. "What a horrid woman," she commented.

Seraphina's laugh was as shaky as she felt. "You do not know the half of it," she said.

CHAPTER TEN

WHEN SERAPHINA RETURNED to the ballroom, Lance immediately knew something was wrong. He always knew when she entered a room, even one as large as this. Somehow, she acted on him like a lodestone. When she was present, he was helpless not to turn toward her.

Even from a distance, he was aware she was distressed and bravely hiding it. As he approached, he could see Mrs. Worthington casting anxious glances at her.

"What has happened?" he demanded.

"Virginia Frogmore accosted our Seraphina," Mrs. Worthington said grimly. "I gave the woman a piece of my mind, but it was upsetting. Stay with her, Lord Lancelot. I am going to find Elaine and Barker."

Lance placed Seraphina's hand on his arm. "Shall I take you to a chair?" he asked.

She walked with him as he headed for a group of empty chairs near the stairs up out of the ballroom, but she protested. "I am not harmed, Lance. Just a little upset. She threatened I would never see the children again, but that is just empty air. It *is* just empty air, isn't it,

Lance?"

She was even more upset than he had at first realized. Her hand quivered, and so did her voice.

"She is talking nonsense, Seraphina," he assured her. "You will get your children back."

She smiled up at him, though her eyes were still wild. "If anyone can do it for me, it will be you, Lance."

Her faith made him feel ten feet tall, but then the Barkers arrived, wrapped her in their affection and concern, and took her home, leaving him with the task of finding each of her partners for the rest of the evening and letting them know that she had taken ill.

By the time he'd made his way around the ballroom, so had the gossip from the ladies' retiring room. Several of Seraphina's disappointed dance partners mentioned that any lady would be ill after such an attack, and the duchess's son, the Duke of Haverford, sent a footman to bring Lance to the entry hall where the duke waited. "I thought you might like the satisfaction of seeing Lady Frogmore's persecutors evicted," he said.

Even as he spoke, the couple were escorted down the stairs from the ballroom by a pair of tall footmen. Marcus Frogmore was half turned away from Lance and the duke, berating the two men.

"I shall tell Her Grace of this outrage. You shall be out on the streets, I can assure you. You have mistaken your instructions, for we have every right to be here. We bought a ticket! Besides, my wife is a particular confidant of Her Grace..." He broke off because his wife was tugging on his arm.

She had been flushed and indignant, and nodding along to Marcus Frogmore's tirade, until she saw the duke waiting at the bottom of the stairs. Something in his face—perhaps it was the expression of chilly hauteur—warned her because she blanched and began grabbing at her husband.

Marcus Frogmore growled, "Just one moment, Virgin..." At that moment, he caught sight of Haverford, and ran out of words.

Before he could find them again, Haverford spoke, his voice as cold as a midwinter northerly wind. "Mrs. Frogmore, you upset a guest in my home. Witnesses tell me that your verbal attack was unprovoked and unforgiveable. Mr. Frogmore, you, and your wife are not welcome at my mother's. Furthermore, you are not welcome in my home or the homes of any member of the Winshire or Haverford families."

Frogmore turned on his wife and snarled, "Virginia, what have done?" Then he turned to Haverford. His voice changed to a wheedle. "Your Grace, she shall be punished, I assure you. There is no need—"

Mrs. Frogmore interrupted. "You told me to catch that little bitch alone and tell her she was—" Her eyes slid sideways to the duke's stern visage, or perhaps to Lance's hasty movement forward, arrested when the duke put a hand in his way. Whatever she had been about to say, she changed it.

"I did what you said," she muttered, with a sullen glare.

Haverford's voice was soft but implacable. "Not another word from either of you." To the footmen, he said, "Escort them to their carriage and make sure they leave the grounds,"

The pair scurried across the huge hall, past the duke, sparing an indignant glare for Lance but saying nothing. They began squabbling again before the door closed behind them.

"Versey, I would be grateful if you would convey to Lady Frogmore my apologies and those of my mother and my stepfather," Haverford said. "We are distressed that she was insulted at an event under our control. Please assure Lady Frogmore that she has our support, and she must let us know if there is anything we can do."

THE FOLLOWING DAY, Lance called on Seraphina for their usual ride. They went to St. James's Park, but the children did not come.

The ride to the park was the one thing he had been able to do for her, and this day, it failed. Elaine, Mrs. Worthington and the other ladies had reintroduced her to Society. Elaine had organized a wardrobe fit for a baroness. Percy, Mrs. Worthington, and the solicitor were solving her legal woes. And Aurelia and Mrs. Worthington had taken up cudgels on her behalf.

All Lance had done was take her to see her children every morning, which was as much for his own sake as hers, since spending this hour with her each day had somehow become necessary to his contentment. Oh. And he had also set his secretary and valet the job of suborning servants in Frogmore's—or, rather, the infant baron's—house. He had not found out anything useful, however. Just that the governess was as nasty as she looked and that the Frogmores largely ignored the children. He didn't tell Seraphina. What would be the point?

Useless. Lance had been useless. He was, of course happy that Seraphina was getting the help she needed. He was grateful to his family and his friends. He would not, could not, be so selfish as to resent them for *being* the help she needed. But he wished there was something that only he could do. Some way of being useful to the lady who was beginning to occupy his every waiting thought.

He drove all the way to the Frogmore townhouse, and there was no sign of the nursery party either heading to the park or away from it.

He needed to find out what was going on. He needed to talk to Hal, his secretary. He took a worried Seraphina back to Elaine's and assured her he would investigate.

"You will let me know as soon as you can?" she asked.

He nodded. "I promise," he said.

When he stepped out of the Barkers' townhouse, both Hal and Lance's valet were waiting by the phaeton with Lance's groom. The valet started forward as Lance came down the steps.

"My lord, trouble at the Frogmores."

"Something wrong with the children?" Lance asked.

"You could say that," said Hal. "Mrs. Frogmore is planning to do a runner and take the children with her. From what the parlor maid overheard, they don't believe the custody hearing here in London will go their way, and they plan to return to the country and apply again to the magistrate who gave them custody and guardianship in the first place."

"They were packing the carriages when we left to find you, my lord," said the valet.

There was no time to be lost trying to hunt down Percy or Barker or someone else Mrs. Frogmore might listen to. "Pile aboard," Lance commanded. "We can talk on the way."

With three in a seat made for two, and the groom clinging behind, they had managed to cobble together a plan by the time they reached the mews behind the Frogmore townhouse. Sure enough, two travelling coaches stood outside the stables, packed high with the luggage.

Thank goodness they were in time. The drivers were not yet in their seats. Men in Frogmore livery lounged against a nearby wall. Lance had been afraid that the detour to his bank might delay them too long, but money was essential to the plan.

"Take the rig a few doors down," Lance told the groom as he dismounted. "We don't want Mrs. Frogmore coming out and seeing it."

"You won't leave me out, though, my lord?" the groom asked. He only left once he had Lance's reassurance.

The other three men approached the loungers. "How would some of you like the rest of the day off and all of you like a month's pay for keeping your mouth shut?" Lance asked.

It took a bit of negotiation, and more money than he had initially offered, but in the end Lance and his men were dressed in Frogmore livery and one of the grooms relieved of duty for the day was on his way to Lance's stable with Lance's team and phaeton.

They were just in time. The word came from the house that they were to drive to the front steps to pick up their passengers.

Lance's groom, with Lance alongside, drove the second carriage after the first. Hal and the valet took the footmen's seat at the rear. As his informants had predicted, Lady Frogmore and her dresser climbed aboard the first carriage, and it trundled away.

The nursery party waited for the second. They pulled up the steps. Hal and the valet leapt down to assist the passengers to board: first the nursemaid with the baby, then the sour governess, and then the two little girls.

They took off after the first carriage, their driver using every opportunity to let the other carriage get ahead—stopping to give way to people, other vehicles, and horses, and keeping their team into a slow walk.

Thankfully, the first carriage took the Windsor Road. It was the logical direction, given that young Baron Frogmore owned a secondary estate just out of Swindon. Lance had hoped Mrs. Frogmore wouldn't risk taking the children north to the principal Frogmore estate in Norfolk, not just because it was obvious, but because a journey of several days would give pursuers time to catch up.

This road would suit Lance's plans very well. He had been thinking about where to hide the children until after the custody hearing made it safe to put them in their mother's hands. Not with any of the Verseys or their closest friends. Percy certainly had the power to refuse to release them, but Lance didn't know how his theft of the children would influence the custody hearing.

It was best if Percy, Lady Frogmore, and Mr. Fortescue knew nothing about it. Then they could swear an oath they had not been involved. It was possible that Mrs. Frogmore would not know they were missing until she arrived at her destination this evening. That would be even better, for it would take at least ten hours to get the message back to London. The custody case could be over before anyone heard that the coach with the children had been hijacked.

However, just in case, Lance planned to take them to someone whose independence would not be questioned.

The turnoff he wanted was forty-five minutes at the slow pace they were traveling. By now, the front carriage was out of sight. Even if the footmen eventually admitted to the part they played in allowing Lance and his men to take over the carriage, they would not know where he had turned off.

The driver picked up the pace on the secondary road. It was only ten minutes later that they turned into the courtyard of Haverford House. He leapt down when the driver stopped the carriage at the front steps. His only concern was the reaction of the governess, but he had a plan for that, too.

He opened the door, put down the steps, and held out his hand. "Miss Hannah," he said. She stood and obediently put her hand on his palm, allowing him to help her down the carriage steps.

She was a miniature version of her mother, with the same warm brown eyes, and the same contained grace. He gave her a reassuring smile as he let go of her hand and she returned a tentative smile of his own that warmed his heart.

He turned back to the carriage for the second child. "Miss Helena." The little girl took his hand without reservation and used him to balance as she leapt from one carriage step to the next and then onto the ground. She then let go of him and skipped to her sister.

Lance held out his arms for the little boy, and the nursemaid passed him over. Little Lord Frogmore made no fuss, just looked up at Lance with wide curious eyes. Blue eyes, rather than the soft brown the two sisters had inherited from their mother. A soft hand brushed Lance's cheek, and the eyes widened still further. Perhaps the little boy had never encountered the slight roughness that was inevitable when a man with a fast-growing beard had not shaved in eight hours.

For a moment, Lance stared into the small baron's eyes. He enjoyed being an uncle, and often spent an hour or even more with his nieces and nephews once they were old enough to play, but he had never before held a child of this age. He had not expected the tender sensations in his breast, nor the yearning for a wife and children. A particular wife. These children.

Little Harry could be mine, if Seraphina would marry me. Hannah and Helena, too.

"Shall I assist the servants to descend, my lord?" Hal asked.

Right. The nursemaid. We are visiting the Haverfords. Lance nodded to Hal and stepped away from the carriage with his charge. Hal offered a hand to the nursemaid, and then to the governess.

"Where are we?" the governess demanded, narrowing her eyes at the magnificent steps leading up to the front door.

"Haverford House, the home of the Duke and Duchess of Haverford," Hal told her. Lance was already carrying Harry up the steps with a girl walking quietly on either side of him, the nursemaid trailing behind.

"I was not informed we were coming here," the governess complained. "Where is Mrs. Frogmore?"

"I am just following orders, ma'am," Hal said. A cunning answer, and the truth, for he was following Lance's orders.

At the door, Lance gave the butler his card, and asked for the duchess, but before the man could respond, the Duke of Haverford strolled down the stairs.

"Lance Versey," he said, "and friends." He smiled at the children. "The Frogmore sisters and young Baron Frogmore, I assume."

"Young ladies, I make known to you the Duke of Haverford. Haverford, Miss Hannah," Lance said, tipping his head to her side since his hands were full, "and Miss Helena," tipping his head the other way.

"Curtsey," hissed the governess, and the two sisters dropped a curtsy. Haverford bowed in response.

"Lord Lancelot has called for Her Grace," the butler told Haverford.

The governess's eyes widened as she looked from Haverford to Lance, but before she could make up her mind whether to ask a titled gentleman why he was dressed in Frogmore livery, Haverford said, "I will show Lord Lancelot and his party up to my wife. This way, Lance."

He led the way up to the next floor and along a wide and elegant passage. The girls hurried to keep up with Lance, and little Harry looked at the passing decor with great interest. From behind him, Lance heard the governess muttering, "I did not know about this stop."

The house was so large, it took several minutes to reach the duchess's private sitting room. Haverford poked his head around the door, and said, "I have some visitors for you, my love." He opened the door wider, and ushered Seraphina's two little girls in. Lance followed.

Haverford stopped the servants at the door. "Please take a chair while you wait," he told them, and closed the door in their faces.

Lance bowed to the duke's wife. "Your Grace, I apologize for calling unannounced."

The duke said, "Lance has, I deduce, come for our help to hide his crimes. He has stolen Lady Frogmore's children back from their wicked uncle."

Helena tugged on Lance's coat. "Have you? Are you going to give us back to Mama?" She had removed her bonnet, and the blond plaits that confined her hair had tumbled down.

"That is my plan, yes," Lance told her. "I hope the duchess might allow you to stay here for a day or two, until it is safe for you to go to your Mama." As if of their own volition, his arms tightened on little Harry, and the boy wriggled. Lance made himself relax. He did not need to protect the children against all comers. Not here in the duchess's private sitting room.

The duchess will have them, will she not? He raised his eyebrows in question, and Her Grace exchanged glances with her husband and then nodded.

"Will we have to wait for very long?" Hannah asked, her voice girlish but her question surprisingly mature. "Harry needs her. We tell him about her every night after the governess goes to bed, but I think he has forgotten her."

"You shall see her soon," Haverford declared. "You do not appear to be worried about Lord Lancelot kidnapping you, young ladies."

Helena shrugged. "We recognized him. He is the man who comes every morning to the park with Mama. She used to hide behind the bushes, and she looked so sad." She drooped her shoulders and poked out a trembling lower lip to illustrate. "We would slow down as much as we dared, but Miss Brant, the governess, would hit us with her switch if we did not keep walking. I do not think Miss Brant ever saw her."

Hannah nodded, and commented, "Then Lord Lance started bringing her, and soon she was not so sad."

Helena continued, "Miss Brant said we would never see Mama again, but we saw her every day. Miss Brant said she had forgotten us, but we knew she had not. We knew she was afraid of Miss Brant and Uncle Marcus, so we did not tell them she came to watch us. When you helped us into the coach today—" she smiled up at Lance—"we knew Mama sent you. I am so glad. I like you, Lord Lance."

Lance had a lump in his throat which needed to be swallowed before he could reply. A welcome interruption allowed him time to recover. Little Lord Harry struggled to be put down, and then set off at great speed across the floor, not so much crawling as wriggling like a caterpillar. His destination was a kitten, who had just stepped out from behind the duchess's couch. The kitten, alarmed perhaps by the intent look in Lord Harry's eyes, shot up one of the curtains, and

Harry stopped, hoisted himself into a sitting position, and looked balefully around the room as if the kitten's escape must be someone else's fault.

Lance had known that, if he managed to persuade Seraphina to marry him, the children would be part of the package. He accepted it as a cost he was prepared to pay. However, in the past half hour, he had fallen quite in love with two brave little girls with Seraphina's eyes and a friendly dauntless boy child not yet a year old. The cost had turned out to instead be a reward. That is, if she would have him.

CHAPTER ELEVEN

S ERAPHINA TRIED NOT to be concerned when Lance did not return that day. He sent a message, which was of some comfort though it was hardly enlightening.

"I found out why the children were not at St. James's Park. They are safe and well. I will be able to tell you more when we next talk. I will hope to see you tomorrow at the hearing."

The note allayed her worry about the children—for she trusted Lance, and if he said the children were safe and well, then they were. However, she fretted instead about Lance's absence. Why could he not come today? He *hoped* to see her at the hearing? Did that mean he might not come?

Had he become aware that she had fallen in love with him? Was he putting a distance between them to protect himself from her embarrassing him with her feelings? Perhaps he wanted to let her down gently? It was probably the second. Lance was such a kind person; he would not want to hurt her.

She begged off from the evening's entertainment, claiming the need for an early night to be well rested for the hearing. But after Elaine, Mrs. Worthington and Barker had left, she wished she had gone, for she found it impossible to sleep. The distraction of an evening out would have at least given her something to think about other than Lance, the children, and tomorrow's hearing.

She wondered how the children were, and whether their keepers had turned them against her, and whether little Harry had any memory of her. She rehearsed the answers to the questions that the solicitor warned her she might have to face on the morrow, and then rehearsed them again and again. She was startled to realize that her thoughts would not stay focused. Instead, she found herself going over and over every interaction with Lance, trying to discover how he felt about her. It was maddening, yet all her concern for her children did not distract her from reflecting on the perfect gentleman who'd taken her under his protection, giving her his devoted allegiance like the knight for whom he was named gave his queen.

Sir Lancelot and his queen loved one another. She tried to squelch the thought. It would not be repressed.

In the early hours of the morning, she heard the Barkers talking softly as they passed her room on the way to their own. She had long since blown her candle out and set her head on the pillow. But still, her worries and her longings would not leave her in peace.

At some point, though, exhaustion must have won, because she woke to the sound of the maid adding wood to a fresh fire. Light shone through the window. It must have been morning, but still quite early. The hearing was not until one o'clock, and how she would keep sane until then, she did not know.

DESPITE WHAT LANCE said in the note, she looked for him all morning, every time the knocker sounded or someone came in the door of whatever room she was in. Eventually, she occupied herself cutting new clothes for her daughters. Cotton gowns in pretty prints had been among those donated by various of the Versey ladies, and these had all had some kind of damage that made them unsuitable for refurbishing for an adult, but there was plenty of material left for a child's dress.

She would have three dresses for each girl ready to try on for a final fit, the size her best guess based on her observations at the park. It was, in essence, an act of hope—a physical representation of her faith that the hearing would go her way, however frail that hope might be.

The trouble was that sewing long seams left her brain ready to continue circling the same topics over and over. When Mrs. Worthington and Elaine joined her, and each picked up a dress to sew, she was even more grateful for their conversation than for their help.

Her two friends kept valiantly introducing new topics until they set the sewing to one side to have a light meal and a cup of tea. Then, at last, they brought up the hearing, proving it had been on their minds, too.

"Seraphina, you are to go with Percy and Aurelia. Aunt Evelyn, you too," Elaine said. "Percy and Barker think it will make a strong first impression on the magistrates."

"You and Barker will follow, of course," Mrs. Worthington said to Elaine. "Seraphina, you will be well supported today."

It was true. When Seraphina entered the courtroom on the duke's arm, it was already crowded with people, many of them Verseys and Versey connections.

Marcus and his supporters were there too, of course—half a dozen men who glared at her as she entered. Apart from Lord Thomas and Marcus himself, she knew none of them.

Fortescue also stood with a group of men she didn't know. He lifted his hand in greeting and gave a slight bow.

Lance was nowhere to be seen, which should not have left her feeling abandoned and vulnerable, for he was only one man, and she had many allies.

The clerk called for everyone to stand, and the panel of three magistrates took their places.

After some initial courtesies, Mr. Fortescue introduced Seraphina's reason for requesting the hearing. "Lady Frogmore seeks a reversal of the custody order regarding her offspring, which was taken in defiance of the custody provisions of her husband's will. She also requests the courts to rescind Mr. Marcus Frogmore's guardianship of her children, allocated by the same court."

He tucked his thumbs into the lapels of his gown. "Your honors, we shall show that Frogmore lied in the last custody and guardianship hearing, that he then evicted Lady Frogmore from her son's house, the son who was still at the time being fed on his mother's milk. Frogmore then refused to allow her to see her children and furthermore, used lies to cut Lady Frogmore off from the income left to her in her father's will."

He went on to talk about Frogmore's debts prior to being granted custody, and his spending since the income belonging to Seraphina and the children fell into his hands.

Marcus Frogmore did not have a solicitor, but made his own speech, in which he denied the charges of lying and assured the judges that he could prove his sister-in-law to be an unfit mother.

One by one, he called up the men who had come with him. Seraphina would not call them gentlemen, for every single one lied, saying she had been intimate with him.

Mr. Fortescue had warned her that this might happen, since Frogmore had used the same strategy at the previous hearing. His barrister, when it was his turn to pose questions, asked each man for details of date, time, and place. "I would like these witnesses to remain, Your Honors," he told the magistrates. "I may have further questions for some of them." The men grumbled, but the magistrates insisted they sit down and stay.

Marcus then spoke as his own witness, asserting that Seraphina was taking money for sexual favors, and offering as evidence that she was fashionably addressed and active in Society. "She has no money, so what other explanation is there?" he asked, rhetorically.

Mr. Fortescue began with the same mild approach she had seen him use, at first, with the trustees. "Mr. Frogmore," he asked, "can you tell the court why you say that Lady Frogmore has no money? Her father was one of the wealthiest men in England, and she is heiress to a princely income." He managed to sound both bewildered and humbled.

Marcus puffed out his chest. "Oh, I stopped her income. Told the trustees what she was like. Told them if she had no income, she'd have to come home."

Mr. Fortescue looked puzzled. "Come home? But your meeting with the trustees occurred while Lady Frogmore was still living at Frogmore Hall with her children." He handed a piece of paper to his clerk who carried it to the court's clerk, who passed it to the chief magistrate.

"That is a copy of the appointment book for Mr. Cranshaw, who was solicitor to Lady Frogmore's father and had been appointed as a trustee for the fortune left to Lady Frogmore and the deceased Lord Frogmore's children by her father. It shows that Mr. Frogmore met with the trustees three days before he told the previous custody hearing that Lady Frogmore had abandoned her children and was cavorting in London."

"And so she was," Marcus blustered.

Mr. Fortescue gave the dates of the court hearing and the meeting with the trustees and asked him to confirm.

Marcus jutted his jaw. His tone was truculent. "I suppose that is correct. What of it?"

"If you might just confirm another detail for me," Mr. Fortescue said. "Were you or were you not deeply in debt when you moved into

Frogmore Hall and took over custody of your brother's children?"

"Not deeply!" Frogmore insisted. "A few tradesmen's bills. All paid off now."

"Would you tell the court how you repaid your debts, and also paid for a number of expensive items in the past six months, since you began receiving incomes on behalf of little Baron Frogmore, Lady Frogmore, and the Misses Frogmore?"

"None of your business," Marcus said, indignantly.

When the magistrates insisted on an answer, he claimed a lucky win on the horses, and then amended that to several wins.

Mr. Fortescue had several more questions about his relationship with his brother, his inheritance from his brother, and why he thought his brother might have left both guardianship and custody away from Marcus.

Seraphina would have said the relationship was terrible, Henry had left Marcus nothing, and the will ignored Marcus in guardianship and custody because Henry didn't trust his brother. Even so, Marcus spun a story about what good friends he was with Henry, and about how she, Seraphina, had seduced Henry into marrying her and then used her wiles to promote a rift between the brothers.

There was a stir in the back of the court as Mr. Fortescue told the magistrates that he'd asked all the questions he had for now. Seraphina glanced toward the door. Her trustees entered, followed by several of the servants from Frogmore Hall, then Seraphina's landlady from Pond Lane.

Lance had also arrived at some point. He was standing right at the back, watching her steadily. When her eyes met his, he gave her a small smile and a nod. She could not help the quirk of her lips in response. Somehow, she felt that matters could not go wrong if Lance was here, projecting his usual confidence. She took a deep breath and sat back in her chair. Even if the magistrates decided against her, it was not over. She knew Lance would keep trying. Surely, in the end, he would prevail.

Seraphina knew the man who stood next to Lance, too. Or, at least, she had met him once. What was the Duke of Haverford doing at her custody hearing?

Mr. Fortescue called his first witness, Mr. Cranshaw. Marcus, back in his seat, folded his hands over his paunch and sent Seraphina a smug grin. The next few minutes wiped the grin off his face.

Mr. Cranshaw, guided by Mr. Fortescue's questions, confirmed the date of the meeting with Marcus, and admitted they had believed Marcus without evidence.

"We have since investigated," he insisted. "Mr. Frogmore's accusations against Lady Frogmore cannot be substantiated, and, in fact, appear to be untrue. Nor can we prove, at the moment, that Mr. Frogmore is misusing income from the estate and the trust. However—"

His voice was drowned out by Marcus, who was on his feet and shouting denials and recriminations.

The clerk and two constables eventually managed to quiet him, and the magistrate promised to have him removed if he interrupted again. "Continue, Mr. Cranshaw," said the Chief Magistrate.

The trustees had been thorough. They had a list of Marcus's debts, though Cranshaw emphasized that there may have been others. Perhaps, but the total was staggering enough as it was! They had compiled a further list of purchases after the Frogmores took charge of the incomes. And finally, Mr. Cranshaw produced a list of places where Marcus Frogmore had been seen losing money in the past few months.

When Mr. Fortescue had finished his questions, Marcus had none. Mr. Cranshaw resumed his seat next to the other two trustees.

"Lord Penningway and Lord Matthew Tewksbury, the other two trustees, are present in the court if the court wishes to hear confirming evidence," said Mr. Fortescue. "Or, if it pleases Your Honors, I can move on to my next group of witnesses."

"Move on, Mr. Fortescue, by all means," the chief magistrate agreed. "We can always revisit the decision if we require further clarification."

The next witness was Seraphina's vicar, to whom she had fled when Marcus had thrown her from the Hall. Mr. Fortescue described him as the spiritual counselor of the people who lived in the vicinity of Frogmore Hall. "Do you know Lady Frogmore?" he asked.

The vicar explained that he had known Seraphina since she came to Frogmore Hall as a young bride, and volunteered, "Lady Frogmore is held in high esteem in the village near Frogmore Hall, as a devoted and virtuous wife and mother, and a good steward of the Hall and the land. She is much missed, and we hope she and the children will soon come home."

Mr. Fortescue then wanted to know whether the vicar had seen Seraphina on a date last October, five days after the meeting with the trustees in London and two days after the hearing in Norfolk.

"Twice," the vicar told him. "In the morning, my dear wife and I met with Lady Frogmore and several others on the church committee to discuss decorating the church for the Harvest Festival. Lady Frogmore asked us to hold the meeting at the Hall, because little Lord Frogmore had been unwell, and she did not want to be away from home in case he needed her."

"So, Lady Frogmore was in residence at the Hall on that date?" Mr. Fortescue asked.

"Why, yes. Ask any of my people, especially the tenants and servants at the Hall. Lady Frogmore was always in residence. From the time Lord Frogmore brought her there in 1808 until the day she arrived on my doorstep, seeking shelter because Mr. Frogmore had cast her out. That was the second time I saw her on the date you mentioned."

The magistrates murmured amongst themselves. Marcus turned

livid and opened his mouth, then caught the chief magistrate's eye and shrank into himself.

The vicar went on to explain that he'd gone up to the Hall to remonstrate with Marcus, who had shown him the door. "A few days later, he and his wife took the children with him to London. My wife and I invited Lady Frogmore to stay with us, where she would be safe. She chose to go to London, to be as near to her children as she could."

This time, Marcus accepted the invitation to ask questions, and tried to make out that the vicar was mistaken about the date. The vicar produced his diary and read out the entry for the day. "I must ask the court's forbearance," he said, blushing just a little, "and apologize to the ladies here present for the strong language I felt impelled to use to describe Mr. Frogmore. It was a private memoir, you understand."

He cleared his throat and read in a voice that carried throughout the room. He started with the date, begged leave to skip his description of the meeting about the Harvest Festival, described Seraphina's arrival, and moved on to declaim:

"As soon as my dear helpmate took our unexpected guest upstairs, I sent the boot boy for my gig, and made my way to Frogmore Hall, where that vile persecutor of widows dared to laugh in my face. He had the gall to suggest—" He glanced up at Seraphina and his flush deepened—"that Lady Frogmore might pay for food and board in a way no man of the cloth would consider nor virtuous widow permit."

He shifted uneasily and lowered his voice so that it could not be heard across the courtroom.

"Repeat that louder, if you please," commanded the chief magistrate.

The vicar leaned forward and shouted, his eyes fixed on Marcus, who shrank back in his chair. "I damned his eyes and called him a scaly jackernapes!" His tone was truculent, as he turned his gaze to the magistrates. "I only regret that my language was not even more intemperate."

After the vicar had been released from the witness stand, Mr. Fortescue asked if the magistrates wanted him to confirm testimony by questioning more witnesses on the same point. Again, they invited him to move to his next group of witnesses.

This time, he questioned the landlady, ascertaining that Seraphina had taken the room in October, arranging to work to pay her for her room. "She worked hard, she did, poor lady. She never had no callers, not of any sort. Not that I allow any goings on, but no one ever came to see her, except at the very last, when she gave her notice and moved, and a man, ever so nice and polite, came to carry her bags for her."

The date the landlady gave for Seraphina's move was a few days before the earliest date given by two of the men who had claimed to have visited her room in the Pond Street house.

At this point, the proceedings were disrupted. A man in Frogmore livery had crept into the room and taken a message to Marcus, who paled, flushed, and leapt to his feet. "It was you," he shouted, pointing across the courtroom at the Duke of Dellborough. "You have taken the children!"

Seraphina found herself on her feet, her head reeling as her heart pounded in her chest. "My children? Where are my children?" Mrs. Worthington put her arm around Seraphina's shoulders and encouraged her to take her seat again. She hunched in the chair, shivering and struggling to breathe. "Where are my children?" she whimpered to Mrs. Worthington.

The noise in her ears was more than just her panic. Everyone was repeating her question. The court's clerk shouted for order.

"What is going on?" The chief magistrate demanded of Marcus and Mr. Fortescue once the room was quiet again.

"I may be of assistance," said Lance's beloved voice, calm and firm, and Seraphina's panic loosened its grasp on her throat. He stepped to the front of the courtroom, and the Duke of Haverford came with him.

Lance introduced himself. "For some weeks, I have had watchers in the Frogmore townhouse," he explained. "I wanted to be able to reassure Lady Frogmore that the children were safe, and to take steps if they were not."

"Bribing the servants?" The chief magistrate asked.

"Indeed," said Lance, without any sign of guilt. "Yesterday, I found out that Lady Frogmore was leaving London with the children. My informants overheard that Frogmore was taking precautions against losing the custody hearing by removing the children from the jurisdiction of this court. Mrs. Frogmore has gone to Swindon."

The words turned into a loud ringing in Seraphina's ears and the courtroom swam before her eyes.

CHAPTER TWELVE

SERAPHINA HAD SLUMPED in her chair, pale as a sheet. Her lips moved. In the hubbub that followed Lance's disclosure, he could not hear the words, but he thought she was repeating, over and over, "My children."

He wanted to go to her. Reassure her. The Duke of Haverford put a restraining hand on his arm. They had discussed this on the way to courtroom. "Do not give Frogmore any reason to suggest anything unseemly in the relationship between you and Lady Frogmore," Haverford had said. "Let others take care of her. We will set her mind at rest soon enough."

"Frogmore!" The chief magistrate did not wait for the clerk to restore order, but bellowed over the noise, and the courtroom hushed to hear him. "Where are Lady Frogmore's children?"

"They—They are meant to be with my wife," Frogmore stammered.

"You attempted to preempt the decision of this court, and now you have lost them," one of the other magistrates accused.

Frogmore rallied at that. "How could I expect justice in a London court when that bitch has Dellborough and his family on her side?"

"Do you dare to accuse this court of partiality?" The third magistrate sounded incredulous, and well he might. If the magistrates had been inclined to give Frogmore any benefit of the doubt, he had just destroyed that chance.

The courtroom waited in spellbound silence for Frogmore to realize that he had shot himself in both feet. In the quiet, Seraphina's broken plea, softly uttered, reached every corner. "My children?"

"If the court will permit," Haverford said, stepping forward, "I can set Lady Frogmore's mind at rest and also reassure the honorable magistrates."

Lance glared at his back. *Get on with it, then. Can't you see how Seraphina is suffering?*

"Very well, Your Grace," the chief magistrate replied, making a hurry-up motion with one hand.

"The carriage containing the children and their servants was intercepted, my lady," Haverford said, "and delivered to my wife. The children are safe and well, and my duchess and their nursemaid are with them as we speak. I am happy to continue to house them and protect them until the court has decided whether to honor their father's will or set it aside in favor of their uncle."

The chief magistrate sniffed and declared he did not believe His Grace's indulgence would be required for long.

Lance barely heard him and paid no attention to the quiet discussion of the magistrates, who had their heads together so they could speak without being heard.

Seraphina was his only focus. She was sitting back in her chair, her clasped hands clutched to her chest, her eyes shining and fixed firmly on Lance. Her smile was tremulous but real, and her lips mouthed the words, "Thank you."

She couldn't know about his part in rescuing the children, so what was she thanking him for? He basked in her smile, anyway.

The magistrates sat up straight in their chairs, looking solemnly out at the crowded room, which hushed immediately.

"The court finds in favor of Lady Frogmore's right to have custody of her children, as appointed in her husband's will," intoned the chief magistrate. "Had His Grace the Duke of Haverford not made it unnecessary, we would now be sending constables to retrieve the children."

One of the other magistrates picked up the refrain. "As it is, we shall order an investigation into Mr. Marcus Frogmore's actions and intentions since his brother died. At first sight, it appears that he was motivated by greed rather than affection for his nieces and nephew, and that he has acted with contempt for the King's law and for God's. An investigation will ascertain the truth. Mr. Frogmore shall be detained for questioning."

Frogmore started to his feet again, but a look from the magistrates caused him to shut his mouth. Two constables moved up, one either side of him, and his eyes darted from one to the other. He flushed bright scarlet and his eyes bulged like a toad's, while sweat poured from his forehead in rivulets.

The first magistrate glared over his glasses at Frogmore's witnesses. "Also, these men who lied to the court and traduced the name of an innocent woman will be given the opportunity to make a true statement before we decide on appropriate penalties." Expressions of dismay from the men were quickly squelched.

The third magistrate took a turn. "One matter remains to be discussed. The guardian appointed in the will is dead. The guardian appointed as a replacement by the court in Norwich has proven unsuitable. The children will be in the custody of their mother, but they need a male guardian. If Lady Frogmore were to marry, the choice would be simple."

The chief magistrate looked across the room directly at Lance. "Lord Lancelot Versey, you have been dedicated in your support for the lady and assiduous in your attentions. May we expect an announcement?"

Lance threw caution to the wind. "I wish for nothing more, Your Honors, but I thought it wrong to court the lady while she was in such trouble. We have not discussed the matter. My affections are fixed, but I have no notion whether the lady returns my esteem."

Seraphina, who was half fainting on Mrs. Worthington's shoulder looked up at that, her eyes widening. A tentative smile trembled on her lips.

"Well, Lady Frogmore?" asked the second magistrate.

Lance opened his mouth to object to the question, but the chief magistrate did it for him.

"Now, now, Wallace, we must not put pressure on the lady. The question of guardian can wait for another day, though until it is settled, the children and their mother will need to live in the household of a responsible and reliable gentleman approved by the court. Lady Frogmore, you are living with the Barkers, are you not? If Lord Barker is willing, you may have the children with you there."

There wasn't a lot more to be said. The magistrates discussed another hearing on the guardianship issue and agreed with Mr. Fortescue that they could make a decision on timing over the next days.

After that, they exited the room through their own private door, the constables escorted Marcus Frogmore from the room, and everyone else was free to leave. Seraphina's trustees bowed politely in her general direction, then hurried away when Percy took a step in their direction. Her old vicar and her landlady hastened to speak to her, and assure her of their support, and some of the villagers, too, took the chance to tell her how the village was not the same with her gone.

Lance hovered patiently, giving them the opportunity to assure her she had friends and supporters. When they went and he was able to reach her, she immediately said, "It was you, wasn't it? I do not know how you did it, but you saved my children."

Haverford abandoned his conversation with Dellborough to say, "He and his servants bribed the Frogmore grooms, borrowed their livery, and took over attendance on the carriage. At the right time, Lance's driver took a turn in the road and drove the children straight to me."

"Not very exciting," Lance demurred.

"So clever!" Seraphina was looking at him as if he had conquered a dragon. "You just quietly magicked them away, and Virginia has no idea when she lost them or where to look. Can we go to them now?"

"I have sent a message, Lady Frogmore," Haverford said. "If you are ready to go home to the Barkers, my duchess and the children will meet you there."

Lance had to admit he was disappointed as the lady who held his heart walked off on Barker's arm. Seraphina had not commented on his proposal? Was it a proposal? He had made his intentions clear, and she didn't react at all. *What did you expect, you idiot? She is desperate to see her children.*

SERAPHINA WANTED TO sing, to shout, to leap about. Her children were safe and nearby. She had won them back. She would have them in her arms within the half hour. Her body yearned to express its joy.

She imagined leaping from the carriage and running to the Barker townhouse. It would not be faster—the horses were maintaining a fast walk—but it would, at least, give her nervous energy something to do!

All that kept her sitting upright in the carriage, with an outward semblance of calm, was a lifetime of being told that a lady did not bother other people with her emotions; a lifetime of unpleasant consequences if she forgot or ignored that rule.

Even so, the Barkers must have realized her inner turmoil, for they did not try to engage her in conversations beyond a couple of remarks. Her answers were rather at random, for she could not think beyond the coming reunion and the man she had left in the courtroom.

Lance didn't really mean it, did he? He proposed to impress the magistrates, Seraphina was certain. What a wonderful man he was, to put himself at risk like that. He would have been in the suds if she'd accepted.

She owed him everything. After all he had already done for her, he had gone even further. He had rescued her children! Would they be angry with her for leaving them with the Frogmores? Would they understand she'd had no choice?

She would have to be patient with Harry. She could not expect him to remember her. She must not rush him. But surely the girls would want a Mama hug? Seraphina had missed Mama hugs so much!

How close were they? Was this the corner? No. They were still streets away.

She was practically leaning out of the window! She cast an apologetic glance at Elaine and Barker expecting them to reprimand her for forgetting her manners.

"I am sorry," she said. "I have been rude."

"Nonsense," Elaine replied. "I am trying to imagine what you are feeling!" She shuddered. "If my boys had been taken away and I got them back... You are very disciplined, Seraphina."

"When our sons are due back from school, Elaine is in a fever of impatience," Barker told her. "She expects their carriage hours before it could possibly arrive and sets the whole household in turmoil making sure that their bed chambers are just so and all their favorite foods are available."

Elaine laughed. "It is true. I miss them so much. Boys must grow up and go away to school. But mothers do not have to like it."

Seraphina returned Elaine's smile. "I do not like to think of Harry going away to school."

"You have some years yet," Elaine consoled her.

Seraphina tried to pay attention, but there was the house, and the carriage outside of it looked grand enough to belong to a duke!

As their carriage pulled up behind it, Seraphina made to open the door, but remembered her place and sat back.

"Go on," Barker encouraged. "You go first. Your children are waiting."

Seraphina thanked him. She could no longer repress her smile, and her eyes were swimming with happy tears. The footman opened the door, and she barely waited for the steps to be lowered before she descended and hurried into the house.

The butler met her smile with one of his own. "They are in the drawing room, my lady," he told her. "Go on up."

She might have levitated up the stairs. She had no memory of traversing the space, all of her mind being focused on arriving. And there they were, her two little girls, leaping to their feet and running into her arms, snuggling into her, all three of them laughing and crying and talking over the top of one another, manners be damned.

"MAY I BEG a ride to the Barkers when you go to join your wife?" Lance murmured to Haverford, just as Dellborough and Fortescue reached him, eager to hear more about his rescue of the children.

"It was nothing," he demurred, as they questioned him about how it was accomplished.

"It was brilliant," Percy said. "I had not thought of putting a watch on the villain, and as for the way you commandeered the carriage! Just brilliant."

Lance shrugged, unaccountably embarrassed but also thrilled that his august and esteemed eldest brother should praise him in such a way. "I wouldn't say brilliant," he objected. "It was only common sense, and not very hard, to bribe a few servants to keep me informed. As for dressing up in livery and driving off with a carriage, that was just opportunistic. I couldn't let Mrs. Frogmore take the children away, after all."

"You must accept, Lance," said Aurelia, in the voice she used for grand pronouncements, "that your entire family is most impressed. Why, brother, you are the hero of the hour. Dear Seraphina certainly thinks so. You must propose to her properly, my dear. We shall be pleased to welcome her to the family."

CHAPTER THIRTEEN

Seraphina glowed with happiness. When Lance and Haverford arrived, she was sitting on a couch in the Barkers drawing room, with a delighted girl pressed tightly against her on each side and little Lord Frogmore on her knee. He was examining her face with wide eyes and one questing hand, which was currently exploring her teeth.

Elaine, with tears in her eyes, whispered, "He just crawled over to her—wriggled, really—and asked to be picked up. Do you think he remembers her, Lance?"

"Perhaps." Or perhaps the sensible little chap knew a good thing when he saw one. If Lance found himself in a room full of strange ladies, he would gravitate to Seraphina, too. He was certain of it.

"Here are Lord Lance and the duke," Helena announced. "Hello, Lord Lance. We have our mother, just like you promised."

Hannah said nothing, but her eyes spoke for her, brimming with joy.

Seraphina looked up from little Harry and turned her beaming smile on Lance. He had to brace his knees, which melted at the warmth she directed his way. "Thank you," she mouthed, then turned her attention back to the child.

Lance forgot that anyone else was in the room, his yearning for this particular woman, these children, consuming him to such an extent that he dropped to the carpet before her. "Seraphina, marry me?" he begged, having just enough wit to keep his voice low. But his words were drowned when Harry recognized him, sent up a crow of welcome, and hurled himself off Seraphina's lap and into Lance's arms.

"He likes you," Seraphina's voice trembled. Had she heard his question? Harry wriggled to be handed back to his mother.

"*We* like Lord Lance," Helena announced.

"He stole us from Aunt Virginia," Hannah informed Seraphina.

Helena added, "We saw him with you at the park, Mama." That led to a conversation about how the children had noticed Seraphina watching them and had been comforted to know that she was nearby and missing them as much as they missed her.

Lance continued kneeling on the carpet while Harry made a game of being passed from Seraphina to him and back again, and the two little girls told their mother all about their rescue.

His second muffed proposal was entirely ignored, as it deserved to be. How Society would laugh if they knew! Lord Lancelot Versey, perfect gentleman, twice asking a lady to marry him under the worst possible circumstances.

Perhaps not the worst—but certainly not conducive to romance! Once in a courtroom and again in the middle of her reunion? He was a complete duffer.

Elaine agreed, after the Haverfords had left and Seraphina had taken the children and the nursemaid up to the nursery. "Honestly, Lance, for a man who is known for his address, you are certainly making a mess of proposing to Seraphina."

"Shows he cares," Barker suggested. "Turns a man's brain to mush, proposing to the woman he loves."

The glance husband and wife exchanged was pregnant with memories, setting Lance wondering about Barker's own proposal, and

Elaine's voice was less scornful when she said, "That is as may be. Go home, Lance. Give Seraphina and the children the night to settle in, then come back tomorrow and propose properly."

LANCE HAD ASKED Seraphina to marry him. Twice. She could explain what he'd said in court as a kindness—yet another action to help her in her quest to regain custody of her children. But falling on his knees in front of, not only his sister and brother-in-law, but also the Duke and Duchess of Haverford? The bald words, *marry me*? That was definitely a proposal.

She fretted all evening about what it meant. She could not let him throw himself away on a person like her, just out of the kindness of his heart. He had done so much for her already. He deserved her gratitude, not to be burdened by her for the rest of his life.

I could look after him. He needs someone who sees him for who he is. Elaine and the others spoke of him as if he was a do-nothing, a nice boy who still needed to grow up and settle down. It made Seraphina so angry. They did not see the good he did, how he influenced others by making kindness fashionable, how he encouraged awkward young men, danced with wallflowers, gave his all to help a desperate mother.

He needs someone who appreciates him. Appreciate was a pale word. She *loved* him. She could be honest with herself. Because she loved him, she could not accept his sacrifice.

Throughout the rest of the day, Seraphina's mind kept darting away to thoughts of Lance, and she had to keep pulling it back to the daughters who clung to her and the son who still thought of her as a pleasant stranger.

Being back with her children was her dream come true. Apparently, though, despite all the sensible warnings she had given herself, she had found a new dream, for Lance's proposal was her last thought that night and permeated her dreams, in which her reunion with her children and her longing for her perfect knight came together in visions of family.

She was up early, awakened when her children came visiting, sneaking from the nursery and down the stairs to her room, which she had shown them the evening before. They carried Harry, wrapped in a blanket, and had thought to bring a fresh clout so that Seraphina could change his wet behind.

Alison, the maid she had been assigned, found all three snuggled in bed with Seraphina, playing a game of "do you remember" about their lives in the country when Henry was alive and far away in London.

"Do you want me to take them back to the nursery, my lady?" asked Alison.

Seraphina, used to fitting in and doing what was expected of her, nearly said yes. But Hannah sighed as she sat up, Helena gave her a look redolent with longing and resignation, and Harry's warm little body was snuggled trustingly against her own. "Let the nursery maid know where the children are," she commanded. "She can bring their breakfast and their clothing here, and they will get ready with me this morning."

Alison nodded as she smiled at the children. "You don't want to be parted from them, and no wonder, my lady. I will be right back, and I will bring you some toast and a cup of tea, shall I?"

They made a merry breakfast of it, with the two maids to wait on them and gossip by themselves in the corner. The scene that greeted Elaine when she knocked on the door was Seraphina marching toast soldiers dipped in egg through the air into the cave of Harry's mouth, while the two little girls giggled over their own eggs and toast.

Seraphina wondered if Elaine would scold, and Hannah and Helena scrambled to their feet to drop a curtsey, looking even more apprehensive than Seraphina felt.

Elaine laughed and borrowed the dressing table chair to join them at the little table. "Good morning, Lord Frogmore, Miss Frogmore, Miss Helena. Sit down, girls, you do not need to stand on ceremony with me. How are you this morning, Seraphina?" She reached for an unclaimed piece of toast.

"Wonderful," Seraphina told her. "Are we not, Hannah? Helena?"

Elaine asked the girls about what they had seen in London—the extent of it appeared to be the inside of the Frogmore townhouse and the walk to St. James's Park Lake and back, until Helena pointed out that they had also been to the grand palace in which the Duchess of Haverford lived.

That led to a conversation about that beautiful and majestic house and its garden. "We were allowed to play in the garden," Hannah confided, "and the duchess played with us!"

"The duke said we were not to slide down the bannisters," Helena said. "He said he got his bottom warmed when he slid down the bannisters."

Helena giggled. "The duchess scolded him for suggesting the idea, and we had to promise we would not try it."

"Yes," Hannah agreed. "For they are very high and long, and it might be dangerous. Also, we might break something."

Helena's face took on a meditative cast. "The bannisters at Frogmore might work."

Seraphina contemplated giving the duke a good scold herself.

The girls were eager to tell Elaine all about what they described as, "When Lord Lance kidnapped us in our carriage." According to them, the governess had sighed and grumbled, but wilted when Lord Lance frowned at her. She had been entirely vanquished by the duchess, who sent her away with one of the servants. Seraphina would have to remember to find out what became of her.

At last, Elaine suggested that the children return to the nursery. "You will see your mother again soon, my dears, but for now I wish to have a word with her." She sent Alison away, too. "Lady Frogmore will need you in half an hour to help her get dressed," she said. "Bring another tea tray then."

Now they would have it. Elaine was going to tell Seraphina not to take Lance's proposal seriously. Seraphina braced herself to deny her own feelings and to reassure Elaine that she did not aspire so high.

Sure enough, Elaine's opening was just what she expected. "Seraphina, I know it is none of my business, but I am going to say something anyway, for I am fond of you both."

"You do not need to worry," Seraphina assured her. "I will not..."

Elaine put up an imperious hand. "Hear me out, please, for I do not want you to make a mistake."

Seraphina subsided, a small part of her wondering if it would, after all, be such a mistake.

Elaine lightly touched Seraphina's hand. "You have to know, Seraphina, that the whole family likes you."

But not enough, apparently, to see her as a fit wife for their brother. And though Seraphina had been telling herself the same thing since yesterday afternoon, she wanted to argue.

"We are all very fond of Lance, but we have never expected much from him," Elaine continued, ignoring or not noticing the rebellion that seethed within Seraphina. How could they not realize how wonderful Lance was?

"We never thought he would marry," Elaine said, "and if he did, we thought it would be to a female without a thought in her head except how to trade on the consequence of his relatives and to spend his money. Instead, he has fallen in love with you, Seraphina, and we are all delighted."

Seraphina stared at her. *Are my ears working properly?* "In love with me?" she repeated. Then blinked while her brain caught up with the rest of that last sentence. "You are?"

"Yes," Elaine insisted. "He is. He asked you to marry him, did he not? In front of other people, too. And we are. You have been very good for him, Seraphina, and for the family, too. We are in the habit of thinking of him as the idle fribble who came down from Cambridge, but you saw a different side of him. You see the hero in him, and he has been a hero for you. You will be kind to him, will you not? You do like him as a man, and not just as a rescuer?"

"But Elaine," Seraphina protested, "He has only proposed out of kindness. He has set out to rescue me, you see, and the magistrates said I needed a husband, and so…"

Elaine grimaced. "I believe you are wrong. But if you must, tell him what you just told me, and see what he says. You *do* love him, I know you do."

Seraphina looked away, but not quickly enough. Elaine crowed, "You do! I can see it in your eyes. I will leave you to get dressed, Seraphina, but do think about what I have said, will you not?"

As if Seraphina could stop thinking about it. Alison returned to help her dress, and she returned random responses to the girl's remarks as her mind went round and round in circles.

She had barely finished when a maid arrived with a message from Elaine. "Lady Barker sent me, my lady. Lord Lancelot has arrived, and Lady Barker asked me to tell you that he is taking you and the children for an outing."

He was waiting in the hall, with a huge bunch of roses, lilies, asters, and forget-me-nots. As he saw her descending the stairs, his eyes widened and his pupils expanded. Affection? Appreciation? Desire? *The last, certainly.* She felt her back stretch under the heat of his gaze, her own core warming, her hips tilting just a little more than was needful to negotiate the stairs.

Perhaps Elaine was right. If he proposed again, she would ask him why. And if Elaine was right a second time, and he really did have some regard for her, perhaps… She did not allow herself to finish the thought, for the dream was ready to explode from her heart and she would not encourage it.

SERAPHINA ACCEPTED LANCE'S floral offering but refused to meet his eyes. He could feel the distance between them, and did not know how to bridge it, especially when the children and their nursemaid came from the back of the hall, all dressed for the outdoors, the girls twirling to show the new dresses their Mama had made for them.

Lance surrendered to the inevitable. "Elaine has suggested that you and I should take the children to Fourniers," he told Seraphina.

Her mystified expression hinted that she'd not heard of the popular restaurant and its associated tearooms. "They sell ices," he explained. "Tea and cakes, too, but I expect that the children would each like to have an ice."

"Ice is cold," Helena observed, "but not tasty. I think I should like a cake."

"You will like these ices," Lance assured her, resolving that she could have a cake as well.

Elaine spoke from the doorway to the front parlor. "I have ordered the landau, Lance. Seraphina, here is Alison with your shawl and bonnet."

The maid handed Seraphina the two items, and took the bunch of flowers. "Please put them in water in my room," Seraphina told her. "They are lovely, Lord Lancelot."

The butler opened the door and Seraphina led the way, each hand holding that of a daughter. The nursemaid followed with little Harry, and Lance brought up the rear. He waved away the waiting footman, and lifted the two little girls, Seraphina, Harry, and the nursemaid up into landau and then clambered up himself.

It was a short ride to Fourniers, made even shorter by the children's palpable excitement. Much though Lance regretted the delay in resolving things with Seraphina, the trip itself was a delight. Hannah and Helena had never ridden in an open carriage, and were excited about everything, and Harry crowed with delight at every animal, whatever their species, age or pedigree.

The tearooms were busy, but a serving maid found them a table. Lance ordered ices for them all, even the nursemaid, as well as a plate of the delicious little iced cakes for which the proprietor, Marcel Fournier, was famous. He sent ices out to the grooms and footmen, too. Even little Harry got his own small dish of ice flavored with the juices of fruit.

"I do like this ice," Helena discovered. "It is tasty, Lord Lance, like you said."

Hannah agreed. Seraphina, who had also never tasted an ice, nodded as she placed a spoonful of it in her mouth, and shut her eyes, the better to savor the flavor. Lance felt her pleasure all the way to the seat of his own, and had to swallow hard and focus on the little girls to keep his body from a reaction that was totally inappropriate in such company and such a public place.

Elaine's idea had been a good one, Lance acknowledged to himself as he helped them back into the landau. Seraphina had relaxed in the company of her happy children. "Thank you, my lord," she said to him. "That was wonderful."

"It was my pleasure," he told her, which was true in so many ways. He loved pleasing the children almost as much as he loved pleasing Seraphina.

The girls chatted happily throughout the trip back to the Barkers. Harry, tired by the outing and the excitement of his first ice, went to sleep in his mother's arms. Lance aided the nursemaid down first, this time, then swung each girl down to the ground and handed her into the care of the nursemaid.

Seraphina bent toward him so she could transfer Harry into his arms, a small warm bundle with the face of a cherub. He carefully laid the little boy into the nursemaid's arms, and she stepped back with him, singing softly as she rocked him.

Lance held his hands out for Seraphina as he had for Hannah and Helena. "I am too heavy," she protested, but she allowed him to clasp each side of her waist and leaned into his grasp as he lifted her down, his eyes on her the whole time, quivering with the effort to place her gently on the ground instead of crushing her to him right there in the street.

Their first kiss, if she allowed one, would be soon, but not outside in the street, in the view of all the world. He offered her his arm and escorted her into the house.

Inside, his patience was rewarded at last. Elaine emerged from the parlor as if she had been lying in wait—and she probably had. She took Harry from the nursemaid, saying, "Hannah! Helena! You must tell me all about your ices! Lance, take Seraphina into the parlor, won't you? Come along, children."

Before anyone could object or even comment, she had swept the nursemaid and children with her up the stairs. Delighted, Lance conducted Seraphina into the parlor and closed the door behind them.

She stared at the door, and then at Lance, her eyes wide. "Lance?"

"I asked Elaine for some time alone with you, Seraphina. Can you not guess why?"

"Oh," she said, and to his dismay cast a longing glance at the door before abruptly sitting down on the nearest chair. "You mean to propose again."

However hard he tried, he could not interpret her tone as encouraging. Nonetheless, he sank to one knee.

She leaned toward him, her hands up as if in protest. "You should not, Lance. You have done so much for me already. I cannot let you sacrifice your chances of a match with someone worthy of you."

His surge of anger was not at her, but at all the people who had convinced her of her unworthiness, with her father and Lord Frogmore at the top of the list. "It is I who am not worthy of you, Seraphina. Your courage, your devotion to your family, your determination, your dignity—they humble me. As for sacrifice—the shoe is quite on the other foot, but I am more selfish than you. You could do much better than the left-over spare of a duke, whose brother has sons and a grandson to take his place. I've never achieved much in my life beyond good manners and a well-tied cravat. I don't deserve you, but I am asking, anyway. If you will have me, I will be the best husband and father that I can."

Seraphina stood to stamp one foot. "You shall not say such things. The left-over spare, indeed! No one could have done what you have done for me. Ever since you gave me hope that day in the park, you have always known exactly the right person to help me, and how to persuade them. If not for you, I would still be living in Pond Street, separated from my children, my reputation in ruins. I am so grateful, Lance. That is why I cannot take further advantage of your generosity."

Lance felt like stamping his own foot. Might have, if he'd not still been on one knee. "Dammit, woman, I am not being generous. I love you."

She sank back into her chair, one hand fluttering over her chest. "What did you say?"

He felt his cheeks heat. "I beg your pardon, Seraphina. Language unbecoming. I don't know what came over me."

She waved his apology away. "Not the curse, Lance. You said… did you really say you love me?" Tears trembled in her eyes, but she was smiling, almost glowing.

"I love you," Lance repeated, hope almost choking the words. He swallowed hard and continued, "I cannot imagine facing the rest of my life without you. Will you marry me, Seraphina? Even if it is just because you need a guardian for your children, let it be me. I will ask nothing you are not prepared to give. Only the privilege of being your husband, of loving you."

She slipped off her chair to kneel before him, slipping her hands into his. "I want to give you everything," she told him. "I love you, Lance."

"You will marry me?" Lance needed her to say the words, so he could start to believe them.

Her smile spread. "I will marry you."

His eyes focused on her lips, turned up toward him, and his mouth lowered almost without his volition. "I am going to kiss you, my love," he warned her.

Seraphina said nothing but lifted her mouth to meet his.

The first touch of their lips inflamed him, and he struggled to keep from hauling her against him. Her awkwardness helped him to retain his senses. She kissed like a complete novice, closed mouth, uncertain what to do.

He set out to teach her, showing her by example all the ways that two pairs of lips could stroke and caress one another. "Open your mouth," he invited, and swept his tongue inside. Aaah. The taste of her. Now he placed her hands on his chest, releasing his own to embrace her.

Not too fast, Lance. Not too much. Don't frighten her.

Her tongue tentatively followed his, and his desire surged, almost overwhelming his control. "My love," he gasped, pulling back to rest his forehead against hers.

The knock on the door gave them a split second's warning, and then Elaine was in the room, followed by Barker and Mrs. Worthington.

Lance stood and assisted Seraphina to her feet. If her knees were as weak as his, she should probably sit down, but first, "Lady Frogmore has agreed to be my wife," he announced.

LANCE SUGGESTED A special license so they could marry within a day, with only immediate family present. Elaine favored banns at St George's, a wedding in four weeks, and a guest list that would be a who's who of society.

Barker asked Seraphina what she thought, since it was her wedding.

"And Lance's," she pointed out.

"It shall be as you wish," Lance told her. "If you want a big Society wedding, my love…"

Seraphina shook her head. People who had been glad to believe Marcus's lies would accept the invitation in order to rub shoulders with her new relatives, and to gawk and stare. She did not want them at her wedding. "A family wedding," she said, decisively. "Family and friends. But is there not a great deal to do?"

"The children and Seraphina need wardrobes of their own, and you will need to decide whether you will live in little Harry's townhouse or Lance's, and make whatever changes are needed for your family," Elaine pointed out.

"You have a few other trivial matters to arrange, too," Barker said. "Marriage settlements, guardianship papers, updating your wills. May I suggest a common license?"

When Seraphina asked, Barker explained that a common license allowed them to marry in a church without waiting for banns to be called. "Many people choose a common license because they do not wish to have their private lives published in the church porch and called out from the pulpit," he said.

Seraphina nodded her agreement with the sentiment.

In the end, they decided on ten days, and what a busy ten days they were!

The trustees, with the Duke of Dellborough leaning on them, resolved to retire and pass their duties to Dellborough, Seraphina's lawyer Mr. Fortescue, and the Duke of Haverford. Percy (Seraphina had to learn to call the duke that, as his family did) suggested Lance, but Lance and Mr. Fortescue thought it best to keep the trust separate from the guardianship of the children. Seraphina was happy to leave that part of it to Lance and his secretary, Mr. Halifax.

Lance was also heavily involved in preparing for his guardianship role. He signed the guardianship papers, which would come into effect as soon as he and Seraphina said their vows. He and Halifax had visited the Frogmore townhouse and collected all of the papers Marcus had left behind. "Hal was shocked," Lance reported. "Apparently your brother-in-law had no discernable system and made no distinction between the barony's business and his own. Hal will sort it all out, though."

"Poor Mr. Halifax," Seraphina said, but Lance insisted that the secretary was in his element. They had already discovered, and put a stop to, Marcus's attempt to sell off all the properties, since they were not entailed to the title. Marcus and Virginia had already disposed of ornaments, artworks, and jewelry from the townhouse, and probably from Frogmore Hall, though the man Lance had sent to check had not yet reported.

Lance had also discovered that Marcus had continued Henry's neglect of the townhouse. "I have a man coming in to look at the roof, and the kitchen desperately needs to be brought into the nineteenth century," he said.

He and Seraphina decided to do it up and live in Lance's townhouse meanwhile. "Once it is habitable," Seraphina suggested, "we could rent it out until Harry is grown. It is his, after all. Your house will be ours."

Mr. Halifax and Mr. Fortescue had drawn up the marriage agreements, consulting with Seraphina and Lance, with a bit of input from Aurelia and Percy. And both Seraphina and Lance had made their wills.

Meanwhile, Seraphina, with Elaine's help, had ordered a whole new wardrobe for herself and for each of the children, had sent in painters to refresh the nursery at Lance's townhouse, and had spent several happy afternoons buying furnishings, books, and toys to fill it.

Then, three days before the wedding, a note arrived from Mrs. Dove Lyon. "Please call to discuss the favor you owe me," it said. "One o'clock this afternoon will suit. Tell no one."

Chapter Fourteen

L ANCE WAITED IN the carriage under protest. He hated letting Seraphina go into the notorious gambling den on her own, though she had entered through the ladies' door at the side, and the place must be nearly deserted at this time of the day.

"*Tell no one,*" Seraphina reminded him. "I don't want her to know I have not followed her instructions, Lance."

Lance scoffed. "What could she do, darling?"

Seraphina said she did not know and she did not want to find out, and so Lance waited. She should be safe enough, and surely Mrs. Dove Lyon would be reasonable? Seraphina had been wise enough to lay conditions on the favor, but, in any case, she now had access to her trust again. She could pay Mrs. Dove Lyon off if the favor was anything she did not want to do.

If the Black Widow proved difficult, Lance would deal with it. He could pay her himself. He could threaten her with the wrath of the Verseys.

He fretted over the possibilities as he waited for what seemed like hours but was really, when he checked his fob watch, no more than twenty minutes. And here she came, escorted back down the side alley by one of Mrs. Dove Lyon's men.

Lance moved away from the window to remain unseen, and a moment later, the carriage door opened, and Seraphina was thanking the man who had just handed her up the steps.

She was frowning slightly but did not seem upset. She put a finger to her lips, enjoining him to silence, and only after the door was shut and they carriage had pulled away from the street did she speak.

"Mrs. Dove Lyon wants me to introduce Moriah Henshaw to Aurelia," she said.

Lance was bewildered. "That is the favor? That is all?"

She grimaced. "It is complicated by the fact that Moriah is Aurelia's niece, or so Mrs. Dove Lyon says. The Earl of Harrowby's grand-daughter."

"It was rumored that an earl was her grandfather, but... Harrow-by?" Lance narrowed his eyes as he recalled gossip that was old when he was first in Society. "Aurelia had a brother who was disinherited for marrying to disoblige his family," he said. He suddenly realized the significance of the widow's intervention. "Are Vincent and Moriah another of Mrs. Dove Lyon's matches?"

Seraphina nodded. "It was Moriah who told me about Mrs. Dove Lyon in the first place. I am not meant to tell you. Mrs. Dove Lyon thinks you might believe your friend is being manipulated."

Lance snorted. "Vincent? She thinks highly of herself if she thinks she could manipulate Vincent! My friend has fallen in love with your friend, Seraphina, and we should help them, if we can."

Seraphina nodded. "She loves him, too. She has had a hard life, Lance, and she is so happy. I don't want to upset Aurelia and Percy, but helping Moriah is the right thing to do."

"Let's send them a note," Lance suggested. "Make a time to meet. We can find out what Moriah wants before we talk to Aurelia."

He was rewarded when his beloved snuggled into his side and said, "Oh, Lance, I knew I could trust you." She lifted her face for his kiss, and they beguiled the return journey to the Barkers in the sweetest of ways.

LANCE CONDUCTED AURELIA to the table where Seraphina waited with Moriah, and then retreated to join Vincent on the other side of the room. Aurelia had chosen the meeting place—the tea rooms at Miss Clemens' Book Emporium.

"Your sister-in-law had better be kind," Vincent grumbled. He hadn't taken his glower off Aurelia since Lance brought her into the room.

"She won't be publicly rude, in any case," Lance assured him. "I thought you said you didn't care whether Moriah's family accepts her or not?"

"I don't," Vincent assured him. "If the duchess and her father come around, then so will my family and Moriah's mother's family. If they do not, we will leave London and be happy together at my country estate. Or perhaps we will travel. Either way, I shall have Moriah, and that is enough to make me happy. But she worries, Lance. She thinks I will miss this life and my family. I will, but if that's the price I have to pay, she is worth it."

"I can't tell you what Aurelia will do," Lance said, "but she has been good to Seraphina."

The cases were different, of course. Seraphina's reputation was a farrago of lies. Moriah's reputation was based on the life she'd been forced to live in order to keep a roof over her head.

"What has happened to Moriah since her parents died is the fault of that old man," Vincent insisted. The Earl of Harrowby had attended Moriah's parents' funeral and told his grieving granddaughter, who was only eighteen, that he wanted nothing to do with her. Moriah had felt fortunate when a suitor offered her marriage, but that good fortune turned to disaster. He died, leaving her mired in debt. Her first protector had been all that saved her from the brothels or worse.

Beyond a doubt, none of it was her fault. Acceptance by her family and Vincent's, and marriage to Vincent, would establish her back in Society for all but the highest of high sticklers. And they would probably contrive to ignore her past for the sake of not offending the two powerful families.

"What's happening?" Vincent asked. "I can't see." A large lady in an extravagantly abundant hat had placed herself at one of the intervening tables.

"Here, swap with me," Lance suggested. "They are smiling at one another. I think it is going well."

In fact, he was sure of it. Before he sat down in Vincent's former chair, he had seen Moriah direct a nod and smile at Vincent.

Vincent's sigh of relief showed how concerned he had been. Even Lance had not been certain—Aurelia had been generous to Seraphina, but she was very straitlaced, on the whole. With the Duchess of Dellborough on their side, Vincent and Moriah would find the rest of Society much easier to handle.

"Seraphina will be pleased you do not have to flee to the country," he commented to his friend. "And so will I. It will be nice to have company while I'm learning to become a staid married man."

"Who would have thought," said his long-time partner in debauchery, "that you and I would be looking forward to such a thing!"

CHAPTER FIFTEEN

IT WAS A quiet wedding, just as Seraphina and Lance had planned. For a time, it seemed as if Elaine would take over and turn it into a magnificent party, with all the Verseys invited, from the smallest child to the remotest connection. "And we shall have to have the Haverfords," she said, "for they were so helpful. Oh, and the Winshires, for they were so welcoming to Seraphina."

Seraphina saw the whole event spiraling out of control, but Lance put his foot down. "No, Elaine. Just a small private wedding. You, Barker, Percy and Aurelia to represent the Verseys. Saxton and his betrothed, because Moriah is Seraphina's friend. Mrs. Worthington for the same reason. And the children. No one else."

Elaine consoled herself with the promise of a big reception for the married couple in two weeks' time, to present them to Society. "One month," Lance insisted.

"My hero," Seraphina whispered to him.

Elaine heard and giggled. "Which makes me the dragon, I suppose?"

She threw her considerable energies instead into plans for entertaining the Frogmore children, who were staying with the Barkers for the first two nights of their mother's marriage. Seraphina was trying not to think about those two nights. Would Lance be disappointed? Henry had been. Henry had said she was cold and boring, and he only came to her because he needed a son. Seraphina had not liked that part of marriage at all.

On the other hand, Henry had never kissed or caressed her as Lance did, and Seraphina definitely did not feel cold when she was in Lance's arms. Moriah assured her that Henry had been selfish and uncaring, which was true, and that things would be different this time. "Trust Lord Lancelot," she advised. "He knows what to do."

She was thinking about tonight again, even as she waited for Percy. He would be her escort to the Grosvenor Chapel, where Lance, their witnesses, and her children waited.

"You look lovely, Seraphina," Percy said, as he walked into the little parlor to which Elaine had sent her when she was ready. Seraphina had thought so, too, when she viewed herself in the mirror. Elaine and her dresser had done a magnificent job.

Seraphina was gowned in rose pink, with roses and pearls twined into her hair. The pearls had been a gift from Lance—several strings of them. With two strings around her neck and two in her hair, she felt very elegant.

She bobbed Percy a curtsey. "Thank you."

"Are you ready to marry my scapegrace brother?" the duke asked.

"Not a scapegrace to me," she retorted, as she took his arm.

"No," Percy acknowledged. "You have been good for him, Seraphina."

In the carriage, he made a few more remarks—just pleasantries that required little of her attention, which was just as well, for Seraphina was busy suppressing her panic. Her mind was jittering from subject to subject. Her mouth was dry and her heart was beating too fast.

Fortunately, it was a short trip to Audley Street. The footman handed her down, and she gladly took Percy's arm again, using his solid presence to give strength to her shaking knees. Then they were inside, and there was Lance, smiling so warmly that all her fears and doubts melted away and she saw only him.

Her last wedding crossed her mind fleetingly, though she had sworn not to think of her previous marriage today. Still, she could not help but compare the two affairs. Both quiet.

The first had been in magnificent St. George's in Mayfair, with only Marcus Frogmore, her father, the vicar and the vicar's wife as witnesses. She had never been in the church before or since, remembered little but an impression of size and magnificence, which made it seem all the emptier. Those who did attend were all grim and cheerless for their own particular reasons. Seraphina had been numb with apprehension, not quite sure what this marriage would mean for her, but frightened it was a change for the worse.

Today, she gathered with friends in the familiar church she had attended since moving to the Barkers, in a building that was still beautiful, but built on a human scale. Everyone was smiling. Her daughters were beaming with joy. Her son crowed when he saw her, and held out his arms, but was distracted when Barker swung his fob watch in front of the boy. Her heart settled as Lance took her hands. He was the reason she was not afraid, this time. Nervous. Concerned that she might disappoint him. Deep down, though, she was confident that Lance would make sure everything turned out as it should.

When it was time to say their vows, his rang out through the church, he proclaimed them with such ardent joy. Seraphina's voice was quieter, but her jubilation was as heartfelt. Then they were wed. The minister presented them to the congregation as Lord and Lady Lancelot Versey, they signed the marriage lines, and the whole group gathered around them, laughing, talking, and conveying earnest congratulations.

They went back to Aurelia's for a wedding breakfast, where

Seraphina was happy to see Aurelia introducing Moriah to Elaine and Barker as her niece Moriah, and to those of the ducal children who joined them as their cousin.

"Aurelia and Percy have been wonderful," Moriah whispered to Seraphina when they had a moment for a private chat. "They took me to visit my grandfather yesterday. Seraphina, he apologized to me! I have never been more astounded. I do not know what Percy said to him, but he certainly seemed contrite."

Lance had been called out of the room by Percy. The pair of them returned, frowning. "What is the matter?" Seraphina asked.

Lance looked around, and then drew Seraphina further away from Harriet and Helena. They were sitting on a sofa, one each side by one of the duke's daughters, who was reading to them from a story book.

"I don't think I told you," Lance said. "Marcus Frogmore was released after he gave his word as a gentleman to appear at the assizes."

Seraphina could see where this was going. "I suppose he has run off," she said.

Elaine and the other adults had joined them. "How silly of the magistrates to believe his promises when the charges against him involve him breaking his word to his brother," she said, with scorn.

Percy nodded. "Lance and I put watchers on him when we heard. He and his wife have boarded a ship and are bound for Italy. I have sent someone for the constables, but we think they will have sailed before anyone can retrieve them."

Seraphina gave a decisive nod. "Excellent," she said. "They will never dare come back to England, for they shall be arrested for running away, and we do not have to spare them a thought for the rest of our lives. I did not expect a wedding present from them, but this is an excellent one."

The men looked surprised, but the women all nodded.

"He deserves to be punished," Lance grumbled.

"He has lost the fortune he thought was his to control, London and all his friends, and his reputation," Seraphina pointed out, then chuckled. "Furthermore, he has to leave his mistress behind him and travel with Virginia which is, I can assure you, a terrible fate."

"Your wife is correct, Lance," said Barker. "Let us forget about those two miscreants. We have champagne punch to drink and a wedding to celebrate."

LANCE DID NOT want to rush Seraphina. Actually, he *did* want to rush her. If she was as experienced as she should have been, as a wife of nearly a decade, he would have had her home to his townhouse and into his bed as soon as the last champagne toast was drunk.

But she was nervous. From the kisses he'd managed to steal so far, he had no doubt about her passionate nature, but he guessed she did. Frogmore had not just been a bad lover. He'd been no sort of lover at all, making a chore out of what should have been a delight.

Lance was determined to take things slow, and that meant waiting until evening before indulging in a quiet candlelit supper, some more caresses, perhaps a bath, and letting things patiently develop.

Step one was to while away the afternoon, which he did by taking Seraphina and the children for a drive in Hyde Park, introducing them to everyone he knew. The fashionable hour had not yet started, but he still found plenty of acquaintances to whom he could say, proudly, "My wife, Lady Lancelot, and our children." They stopped to throw bread to the ducks, an activity that Harry demanded to join until Lance squatted so the little boy could balance between his knees and hold out a piece of bread.

When an audacious duck hurried up to grab it, Harry squealed, hurled the remaining crust at the interloper, and attempted to climb

Lance. He watched the remainder of the show from high in Lance's arms.

Next, they bought ices again, this time from Gunter's. Finally, he drove the landau back to the Barkers. It was nearly five o'clock. Near enough to evening, surely?

"Now you remember I am going to stay with Lance at his townhouse tonight," Seraphina said to Hannah and Helena, as they waited in the entry hall for the nursemaid.

"Yes," Hannah replied. "We are staying with Auntie Elaine and Uncle Barker for two nights, and then we are coming to live with you at Papa's townhouse."

The girls had been calling Lance "Papa" all afternoon. Each time he heard it, it took his breath, and his chest felt two sizes too large for his waistcoat.

"We will not see you tomorrow, because people who have just married need time on their own, Auntie Elaine says," Helena reported. "But you will come for us the next day, and then we will all live together like a real family."

"We *are* a real family," Lance assured them, and Seraphina held out her arms for the girls. They both had a hug, then one by one held up their arms for Lance, who shifted Harry and squatted down so he could hug each of them in turn.

The nursemaid waited to take Harry from him. "Nursery tea time, Lord Harry," she said, cheerfully, as the little boy buried his head in Lance's shoulder and refused to move.

"Ngum, ngum, Harry," Helena encouraged. Harry opened one eye to peep at his sister, and Hannah and Helena mimed eating something that was seriously pleasurable.

Harry lifted his head to consider the matter, planted a smoochy kiss on Lance's cheek, and allowed himself to be transferred to the nursemaid. "Ngum!" he commanded.

Elaine appeared and waved Lance and Seraphina on their way.

"Off you two go. We will all be fine, won't we girls?"

Lance took Seraphina's hand and led her out to the carriage. "Elaine will look after them," he assured her.

"And you will look after me," his lovely wife replied, with only a slight quaver in her voice.

Just as well they were in an open carriage, for he would have had to kiss her at that, and he had a whole seduction planned.

It started when they arrived home. The butler nodded at their appearance, and a footman raced off to order the water that had been heating all afternoon. In less than fifteen minutes, they would have a hot bath to share, in the huge tub that Lance had installed in the bathing room upstairs. Hot water still had to be carried, but cold water was piped to the room, and a drain took away the waste when the plug was removed.

The supper he had ordered would be waiting for them in his room when they had finished bathing. A cold supper, in case they did not get to it straightaway.

But first, something to calm her nerves. He conducted her through to the drawing room. "Would you like another champagne, my love? Or perhaps a sherry?"

"A little port?" Seraphina asked. "I know it is early, but…"

"It is just before bedtime," Lance assured her, his voice huskier than he intended.

Her eyes widened and she gulped. "It is?"

Lance swallowed, smoothing his voice as he said, "I have ordered a bath, and supper will be served in our rooms." He took her a small glass of port. "I wish to make love to you, Seraphina. I want to worship every inch of your body, though we can wait if that is what you prefer." *Please, please, please don't say you prefer to wait.*

She met his eyes, her own apprehensive but determined. "I want you to make love to me, Lance. I am a little nervous, but only because I am not very good at this. I do not want you to be disappointed."

"I won't be," he assured you. "It is not a performance, my love. It is a conversation; your actions speak to me and mine to you. There is no right and wrong. No marks to be awarded." He drew her back to her feet, took her empty glass and placed it on a table out of the way. He then dropped a series of kisses across her lips and along her jaw to her neck, saying in the gaps between kisses, "It is me telling you with hands and lips and other parts of my body that I adore you. It is you telling me, with sighs and moans if you have no words, that you like what I am doing."

He undid the buttons on her pelisse, clearing the way to kiss down her throat. "If it pleases you to do so, your hands and lips can answer mine, and I will tell you what pleases me, though I suspect, beloved, that it will be everything."

He had her pelisse off, now, and was deftly slipping the buttons of her dress from their moorings. He would give her a foretaste of pleasure, he decided, and ease her trepidation. "You will please me." He had loosened the laces of her stays enough to lift one breast from its cradle. "Just being with you pleases me. Touching you like this pleases me." He licked in a circle around the nipple and then across it. "Because I love you, Seraphina."

He pulled back, suddenly serious. "When we two become one, my wife, it will be new for each of us. Neither of us has made love to a spouse. You were wed to a cretin; I have taken transitory pleasure from a series of women I paid in money or gifts. Neither my past nor yours has given us any idea what to expect. I can only tell you that what I have experienced with you so far is beyond anything I have ever known."

"Truly?" she asked, reaching up to place a gentle hand on his jaw, her eyes shining, "for it is the same for me."

After that, there were no further words beyond a fervent, "Oh yes," and a moan or two. Lance's plan for a slow seduction was shelved as his darling gained confidence in her own power over him.

And their first time together was not upstairs in the bed they would share for the rest of their lives, whenever they were in London, but on the sofa in the drawing room, both of them still half-dressed.

Afterward, they crept hand in hand through suspiciously empty passages (which was as well, for their garments were rumpled and still partly undone). The bath water had cooled. Lance ordered more hot water and fed Seraphina strawberries dipped in champagne and chocolate bon bons from Forniers while they waited.

Their second time was in the bath. Seraphina was proving to be an excellent student. At last, after an intimate supper to recruit their energies, they managed to make love in the bed.

They lay, still tangled together, Seraphina's head on Lance's shoulder. "It cannot be like that for everyone," Seraphina marveled. "No one would ever get anything done!"

"It isn't," Lance assured her, "but it will be like that for us."

And it was.

THE END

Author's Note

As well as being a contribution to the Lyon's Den series, this book is a retelling of a fairy tale. My frog princess finds her own determined way from Pond St. to a man who can help her enter Society. He is bound by a promise to help her, though he feels the same initial horror at the thought as the princess in the original tale. Like that original frog, my Seraphina needs certain acts of acceptance from her chosen champion in order to belong in the Polite World. He is seen in public with her. He eats supper with her at a ball. He dances with her. In the end, but only after they are married, they share a bed.

You will catch glimpses or hear mention of other characters from my books, but two of the characters who play an important part in the story are not mine. Vincent Lord Saxby, Lance's friend who is with him on the night of the fateful wager, and Moriah Henshaw, who first told Seraphina about Mrs. Dove Lyon, belong to Sherry Ewing, and are the hero and heroine of her Lyon's Den book, *To Claim a Lyon's Heart*.

I'd also like to mention that you'll see my characters occasionally using Regency slang. For example, the term *bosky* was one of many expressions that meant drunk. *A trifle disguised* was a little drunk. *Ape-drunk* was very drunk. Or the word cattle, which describes a team of horses and not oxen as one first envisions. These terms are some of many that appear in the Regency novels of the great Georgette Heyer.

In her research, Heyer read many letters, diaries, and other un-published papers of people who actually lived in the early nineteenth century and found a lot of terms that were no longer use by the time she was writing just over a century later. Some of them have also been collected by other researchers. Many haven't.

She even claimed to have invented a few to catch out those who plagiarized her books and her ideas. (*Bosky* isn't one of those. According to Books Ngram Viewer, which scans published documents that have been digitized, bosky was in use by 1618, and its frequency of use climbed from about 1750.)

Here's a resource that lists the expressions you might find in her pages and those of her many author admirers: www.georgette-heyer.com/slang.html

About the Author

Have you ever wanted something so much you were afraid to even try? That was Jude ten years ago.

For as long as she can remember, she's wanted to be a novelist. She even started dozens of stories, over the years.

But life kept getting in the way. A seriously ill child who required years of therapy; a rising mortgage that led to a full-time job; six children, her own chronic illness… the writing took a back seat.

As the years passed, the fear grew. If she didn't put her stories out there in the market, she wouldn't risk making a fool of herself. She could keep the dream alive if she never put it to the test.

Then her mother died. That great lady had waited her whole life to read a novel of Jude's, and now it would never happen.

So Jude faced her fear and changed it—told everyone she knew she was writing a novel. Now she'd make a fool of herself for certain if she didn't finish.

Her first book came out to excellent reviews in December 2014, and the rest is history. Many books, lots of positive reviews, and a few awards later, she feels foolish for not starting earlier.

Jude write historical fiction with a large helping of romance, a splash of Regency, and a twist of suspense. She then tries to figure out how to slot the story into a genre category. She's mad keen on history, enjoys what happens to people in the crucible of a passionate relationship, and loves to use a good mystery and some real danger as mechanisms to torture her characters.

Dip your toe into her world with one of her lunch-time reads collections or a novella, or dive into a novel. And let her know what you think.

Website and blog:
judeknightauthor.com

Subscribe to newsletter:
judeknightauthor.com/newsletter

Bookshop:
judeknight.selz.com

Facebook:
facebook.com/JudeKnightAuthor

Twitter:
twitter.com/JudeKnightBooks

Pinterest:
nz.pinterest.com/jknight1033

Bookbub:
bookbub.com/profile/jude-knight

Books + Main Bites:
bookandmainbites.com/JudeKnightAuthor

Amazon author page:
amazon.com/Jude-Knight/e/B00RG3SG7I

Goodreads:
goodreads.com/author/show/8603586.Jude_Knight

LinkedIn:
linkedin.com/in/jude-knight-465557166

Printed in Great Britain
by Amazon

23836658R00089